# ALONE

## Book 6:

## On Desert Sands

D1522836

By Darrell Maloney

This book is dedicated to:

My mother and father, Frances and Troy Maloney.
The finest people I've ever known.

Thank you for everything.

## The Story Thus Far...

Dave and Sarah Anna Speer had been preppers for years. They didn't know what was coming, exactly. But they knew it was big, would be felt around the world, and would last forever.

Or at least a very long time.

So they prepared. They planned for everything, with backup plans for their backup plans.

The one thing they couldn't plan for was the timing of the event, whatever it was.

And their timing couldn't have been worse, for on the day when the electromagnetic pulses struck the earth and brought everything to a screeching halt, they weren't even together.

It happened on the very day Sarah took their daughters a thousand miles away, to Kansas City, for a wedding.

Dave was alone, and didn't even know if his family had survived their trip.

He traveled to Kansas City to find them, only to find out they were being held captive by a brutal escaped convict named Swain.

Dave went to war, using guerilla techniques he learned in the Marine Corps to whittle down Swain's private army one by one.

As well as tactics which were his alone. Things not even the Corps would dare try.

He was successful in killing all of the captors, except for Swain himself.

Dave would never ask what Swain did to Sarah. He respected her enough not to. But he could see from the fire in her eyes how much she hated the man. And he was certain of two things. He didn't *want* to know what had happened between the two. And Sarah deserved the right to exact her own vengeance.

"I want to kill that bastard myself," Sarah told him. "I deserve the pleasure."

And dispatch him she did, directly into the fiery pits of hell.

The siege was over.

But not the sorrow.

"Where's Beth?" Dave asked about his youngest daughter.

"They took her. Several months ago."

"What do you mean, they took her?"

"An older couple. They had a Red Ford Ranger pickup they took the engine out of. They built a floor and bench into the engine compartment and turned it into a horse-drawn vehicle."

One of Swain's men sold her into slavery.

For seven pieces of silver.

Little Beth, now eight years old, was out there somewhere.

And it was up to Dave to find her.

Once again he was all alone, and back on the road. This time following the only lead he had.

That the couple had headed toward Albuquerque several months before.

He left Sarah and Lindsey with trusted neighbors before he left. He didn't have to worry about them. At least not for now. They were in a heavily fortified underground compound. One seemingly impenetrable.

He could focus on finding Beth, taking her back, and punishing those responsible for taking her.

Dave knew nothing about them. But he planned to kill them.

For they'd taken his baby and were doing God-only knew what kind of horrific things to her.

That was all he really needed to know.

As the last chapter drew to a close, Dave arrived at the outskirts of New Mexico's largest city to find it had been taken over by gangs and thugs. He was told he could go in. But he'd never be allowed to come back out again.

He had a plan. A plan not only to get into the city, but to be introduced to the movers and shakers who ran the place.

Those who could help him find the kidnappers and get his daughter back.

But he needed the assistance of someone to make his plan work.

Someone he'd never have associated with before the power went out.

Someone he'd once have despised.

But who now would be his closest ally.

It was, as he saw it, the only chance he and little Beth had.

**And now, Chapter 6 of the Alone series...**

**On Desert Sands**

## Chapter 1

*Three months before, when Dave Speer was still in San Antonio, preparing for his journey to find his missing family...*

They'd just left Albuquerque and were headed west, their final destination the high desert of California.

Old Sal hadn't been home in almost forty years. Nellie a bit longer than that. She hadn't gone with him the last time because she was pregnant with their first child and had been visiting her mother in Dallas when she went into labor.

"It can't be labor," she protested to everyone within earshot. And even some not. "I'm only seven months along!"

But babies come when they want to. At least they did back then. In 1976 there weren't as many fancy gadgets to tell doctors when to induce labor and when to try to delay it.

And seventy tortuous hours later Salvatore Ambrosio Junior was born. All ten pounds one ounce of him. With a full head of jet black hair, just like his father. And the cutest dimples he got from his mom.

Nobody told Vito, as he came to be called, that babies aren't supposed to be two months early. And it wouldn't have mattered much anyway. Vito was as hard-headed as his father and high strung as well.

The doctors told Nellie it was a good thing she did have him early. If she hadn't he'd have been thirteen pounds, maybe more. And she'd wear a C-section scar the rest of her life. If she survived the procedure at all.

As it was, the strain of baby Huey did its own damage, and she was told immediately after the birth not to expect any more.

That saddened Sal and Nellie, but they learned to accept it.

Little Vito, with no brothers or sisters to share his parents' attention, was raised with everything he needed. And most of what he wanted. He was a bit spoiled, but not so much it hampered his ability to make others like him.

At twenty two, fresh out of college and ready to conquer the world, he met and fell in love with a girl named Melissa.

Both were journalists, he in print media and she in television. Both were considered rising stars in their respective professions. Their bright future seemed assured.

In 2007 their one and only child was born. A girl, as smart as she was pretty, with curly hair and a smile that would melt even the coldest heart.

Her birth certificate said Rebecca. But everybody called her Becky.

The story of Salvatore Ambrosio Jr. and his lovely wife and daughter would likely have ended in fairy tale style were it not for a series of tragic events.

The first was a series of massive storms on the surface of the sun on, of all days, Becky's seventh birthday.

The exceedingly rare storms were the worst in more than two hundred years. And the first since planet earth had gotten technologically advanced.

That in itself wouldn't have affected humans much were it not for the massive electromagnetic pulses it sent streaming toward the earth.

Similar storms in the early-1800s sent an almost identical array of pulses. They did almost no damage at all. Some sensitive farm animals fell over and threw up. Some sensitive humans felt nauseated or dizzy.

But it didn't affect machines because machines weren't yet powered by electricity.

In 2014, however, darned near everything was.

That was the first tragic event which changed the Ambrosio family's fairy tale existence.

The second was the murder of Vito and Melissa, by a band of marauders a few months into the blackout. Someone had told them the house on the corner of the street had a hoard of gold coins worth tens of thousands of dollars.

The trouble was the informant wasn't very good with directions. He sent the thieves to the southwest corner of the block. Vito tried to reason with the men. To explain that no, they had no gold. They had never thought to keep any. They hadn't foreseen the blackout and thought their money was safe in the bank.

Vito was shot in the back of the head, execution style. The band of thieves thought that would loosen Melissa's tongue and she'd turn over the gold.

But there was no gold to turn over. They settled for abusing her in a dozen different ways before mercifully putting her out of her misery by shooting her too.

The man across the street on the *southeast* corner of the block was tucked safely in a barricaded basement and unable to hear the gunshots as he blissfully counted his gold coins.

The third and final insult to the Ambrosio family was perhaps the most heartbreaking.

Young Becky, not sure what to do or who to trust, covered the bodies of her parents with blankets and continued to reside in the house.

As the days went by, the stench of decaying human flesh forced her to camp in the back yard. That was a relief, but not much. For there were corpses rotting all over the neighborhood.

The days turned to weeks, and each day young Becky read to pass the time and prayed that her grandparents would come to rescue her from that vile place. Her water supply ran out, and she drank water from a small stream in a nearby park. It made her throw up and gave her diarrhea, but she didn't associate the two to have a connection and drank even more water to quench her thirst.

She was afraid to venture away from the house. She knew the world was full of very bad people. When her food ran out she started eating cans of dog food she found in the garage.

One night she was stung by a spider and her arm began to swell. She developed a fever and grew lethargic. She stopped eating and stopped going to the creek for water.

The infected bite was a vicious thing. It raised her temperature to an almost comatose level and made her hallucinate. She dreamed her mother was leaning over her, caressing her, telling her everything would be okay.

In her last moments she tried to cry. But her body was too dehydrated to form the tears.

Instead, she made a final prayer. For God to take her wherever her mommy and daddy were.

## Chapter 2

Sal Senior and Nellie lived only forty miles away. They were old now and hadn't exercised in years. But they could have covered five miles a day on foot, and would have been there in a little more than a week.

They simply didn't know they were needed.

They, like everyone else, tried to wait patiently for the electric company to restore the city's power. For someone to come out and explain to them what kind of power outage could short out their vehicles too.

And then to tell them how to get their vehicles started again.

Word traveled painfully slowly with no television, no radio, no telephones.

It wasn't until the fifth day that old Sal finally admitted what Nellie had accepted two days before: that the power was likely never coming back on.

Under other circumstances Sal and Nellie would have felt an overpowering need to get to the children and to help them get through whatever had caused this catastrophe.

They'd have packed a couple of bags with food and water, and perhaps a spare pair of shoes. And they'd have struck out toward Vito's house a few painful miles at a time.

But Vito was a strapping man. He was in the prime of life and in wonderful shape. Melissa saw to that. She made him eat healthy foods, and in reasonable amounts. She took him jogging at night while Becky followed close behind on her bicycle. He had a good head on his shoulders.

Sal and Nellie had every reason in the world to believe that Vito could keep his family safe and provide for them during this terrible time.

It just never dawned on them that six heavily armed men might rush the house and overpower their son.

They were making plans to join Vito and his family, but thought they had all the time in the world to get there.

Sal Senior had been a backyard mechanic his entire life. And he and Nellie happened to live on a farm just outside the city limits. So they had a couple of horses.

They also had a Ford Ranger pickup truck in candy apple red.

Once Sal finally admitted that his pickup truck would likely never run again, he decided to give it a second chance at life.

It wasn't easy. Without power tools to aid him he had to do things the old fashioned way. With hand wrenches and a whole bunch of elbow grease.

He had a manual hoist out behind the barn, and with the help of a neighbor was able to get the engine out. Then the transmission. He concocted a handy little pivot which made the front wheels turn with the horses. Then an outrigger to fasten the horses to.

On the floor of the engine compartment went two sheets of plywood, cut to fit perfectly. A bench seat atop of that, and a homemade braking system.

Oh, and he kicked out the windshield too.

Nellie threw a fit about that part, but he explained.

"We'll be traveling in hot weather. I could break out the side windows to give you a breeze, or I could break out the windshield. The window on the back of the cab slides open, so you can adjust it accordingly. And this way I can talk to you, my dear wife, while I drive the rig."

"Is that what you're calling this thing, Sal? A rig?"

"Well, it ain't really much of a truck anymore, now is it?"

"No. I suppose not. But what about when it rains?"

"Well now, if it rains, I damn sure ain't gonna be sittin' on that bench driving. When it rains we'll cover the open windshield with a plastic tarp and wait for it to stop."

In the end, Nellie was impressed. The rig certainly wasn't much to look at. But it would get them where they needed to go.

And it certainly beat walking for forty miles.

It turned out that everyone else who saw the rig was impressed with it as well.

Several offered to buy it and the team of horses.

"No thank you," Sal said each time. "I'm too old to walk. Besides, my granddaughter will get a kick out of helping me drive it."

## Chapter 3

As they'd turned up the street that fateful day so many months before, Sal had been beaming with pride. A father is always proud of the things he can do to impress his son, and he couldn't wait to take Vito around the block in his new pride and joy.

But it wasn't meant to be.

Sal knew the moment he stepped onto his son's front porch.

Looters had kicked in the front door to see what goodies were inside, then were repelled by the stench.

The horrific smell still permeated everything, and wafted out the broken door as though it were a great monster forbidding entry into a vile and truly evil place.

The smell of three bodies being slowly turned into dust.

It was a disgusting task for the old man. Especially his son and daughter-in-law, for they were mostly bones now. Bones and an indiscernible pile of muck. Becky was a bit easier, because her bones didn't fall free when he went to pick her up. And because she'd had the courtesy to wrap herself up in a blanket just before she died.

Yes, it was an incredibly disgusting task. But the old man would do no less for them. He failed them in life, not being there to help protect them. He wouldn't fail them in death.

Digging the graves put a toll on him. At that point, all the dogs hadn't been eaten yet. But many were set free just before their owners committed suicide and were now running around in packs.

There was no way any damn dogs were digging up his loved ones. So even though he risked a major heart attack, he spent seven hours on that unusually hot summer day, digging two graves that were six feet long, three feet wide, and six feet deep.

Little Becky's went a little quicker because he cut the dimensions by half.

They sang *Amazing Grace* and *Shall We Gather at the River* and he prayed over the graves.

It was just after that when Nellie's mind went. She fell into a funk, not saying a single word. All the time staring into space, into nothingness. Even when Sal held her face in his hands and looked into her eyes he saw nothing. A living, breathing person, sure. But one whose soul seemed to have left her.

That phase lasted roughly two weeks. Sal didn't want to return home. There were too many memories there. Everywhere he looked, he'd see visions of better times. Every time he walked up the stairs, he'd remember how little Vito would haul out his G.I. Joes and use the staircase to play war games. Every time he sat at the dining room table he'd remember playing Old Maid with little Becky. Every time he'd go to the back yard pool to fetch more water he'd remember the pool parties. All the laughing and fun and the neighborhood kids playing Marco Polo.

No, they'd never go back. It would be too painful now.

So they wandered, as many others started to do. During the days, they rode their rig down the nation's interstates, heading in no particular direction. He on the wooden bench in the Ranger's engine compartment, not unlike an old west wagoneer. She sitting quietly on the driver's seat, staring at nothing and feeling nothing. Sometimes resting her head on the now-worthless steering wheel to nap.

Nellie eventually came back to the world of the living. But she never came back to being normal. Her madness simply entered a new stage as she wept at the drop of a hat and constantly called out for Vito and for Becky. Strangely enough, she never called for Melissa, though they'd been as close as two in-laws could be.

It was during this stage that Nellie became delusional and was convinced they'd never found the bodies or buried them. That they were still on the road, on the way to Vito's house in the city.

That Vito and Melissa and little Becky were still alive and well.

It was then that Nellie would call up to Sal in his driver's seat at least twenty times a day.

"How long before we get there, honey? I can't wait to see them again. Will we be there soon?"

It broke Sal's heart every time she asked. For although he showed none of the outward signs of grief as Nellie did, he was hurting too.

They'd traveled three states that way, driving the rig by day and camping at the roadside by night. They'd frequently stop at Walmart trucks, as all the other highway travelers did, and pick through them to find what they could use.

A case of chili and a case of Ravioli could last them a week or more. And there was always at least a pallet, sometimes two, of bottled drinking water.

Old Sal, with plenty of time to think, decided it wasn't really a bad way to live. They slept under the stars each night, on a mattress in the back of their truck which was covered with boxes and personal items when they traveled. Sal unloaded everything from the mattress each evening, stacking it neatly beside the truck. And he and his wife of thirty seven years would lay there, her head on his shoulder, and look at the stars and the moon.

And the clouds rolling by.

She seldom said anything even now, after she started speaking again. She mostly just watched and listened to Sal's heart beating.

Sal looked at the heavens each night and wished things could go back to the way they used to be.

No, it wasn't a bad way to live. They had enough to eat and drink, without foraging through empty supermarket shelves or having to plant gardens like survivors in the city had to do.

And they didn't have to worry about gangs of marauders going door to door to rob and cause havoc, as the city dwellers did.

As Vito and Melissa and little Becky did.

Highway travelers were a different breed, Sal was finding out.

They knew that food and water were plentiful, so they didn't have to steal from one another. And most of them were willing to help if called upon. Or to carry on a conversation with a man who hungered for the sound of another human voice.

## Chapter 4

Sal parked his rig behind a Walmart truck one afternoon and rooted through it, setting aside two cases of drinking water and three cases of Campbell's Chunky Soup. He was getting ready to leave when a young woman appeared out of nowhere.

"Hey there, old timer. Did you see any jewelry in there?"

"Jewelry? Never thought to look for any. You can't eat jewelry."

"Nope. You can't. But gold comes in pretty handy these days when you need other things that you can't eat."

"Really? Like what?"

"Well, like for example, that horse-drawn pickup back there. That's yours, isn't it?"

"Yes."

"Pretty clever."

"Thank you, ma'am."

"Say one of your horses comes up lame. Or dies of a heart attack from pulling a heavy vehicle it's not used to pulling. How are you going to replace it?"

"Never really thought of it, to be honest."

"It's something you should think about, old timer. Horses don't live forever. And while there are plenty out there available, they don't go cheap. That's why you should be collecting jewelry from these trucks."

"I never thought of that, but it makes sense, Miss…"

"Call me Julie."

He reached out his right hand and she shook it.

"To be honest, Julie, I never once thought that one of my horses might die on me. And I certainly never thought there might be gold in these trucks. I thought Walmart only sold costume jewelry."

"Nope. They sell gold chains and engagement sets. And a lot of it's pretty good quality. No self-respecting woman is going to let her man go cheap on her engagement ring. They sell diamonds too. But nobody will accept diamonds for a horse purchase. Too much chance of getting ripped off."

"What did you do before the blackout, Julie? Were you a financial advisor? Maybe a precious metals dealer?"

Julie laughed. It came easy and made her pretty face even more so.

"Oh, no. I was a repo chick. When people got behind on their payments and the banks were on the hook, I went out and collected their cars. Boats too, sometimes."

"That sounds like an interesting line of work."

"Yep. It can be. Your rig says you're headed north. Any chance you'll take on a rider?"

Sal was caught short. Many people had offered to buy his rig since he left home. But no one had ever asked for a ride before.

But he didn't hesitate. Julie the repo-chick seemed genuine, and he hadn't heard a peep from Nellie for three days. He was starved for human conversation, and he didn't think Nellie would mind.

Julie spent three full days, riding on the bench seat next to Sal, taking her turns driving the team. Along the way she showed Sal how to find the unmarked boxes which contained the jewelry, and they split the take fifty-fifty each time.

"Put it aside, but hide it very well. The day will come when you have to replace one or both horses, and gold, silver and penicillin are the only acceptable forms of currency these days."

After the third day Julie the repo chick said her goodbyes, having to turn east to wherever she was headed. Old Sal hated to see her go, for by that time she'd become a friend.

"Be careful," he said as she started to walk away. "And thanks for the advice."

"No problem, old timer. You take care of that wife of yours. She's really having a rough go of it."

"I will. I promise."

Nellie seemed to be getting worse by the day. Sal was afraid he might lose her permanently. Not in body, for she seemed to be in good physical health. But her mind was slipping farther and farther away as each day went by.

A week later, just as Julie had suggested, one of the horses began to favor one of his front legs. Sal examined it and didn't find anything wrong with the hoof. Nothing wrong with the leg either. At least what he could see. The knee joint was swollen, but wasn't much bigger than the joint on the other side.

But the horse jerked when Sal poked and prodded on the joint. It was then he realized it wasn't much bigger than the other one because both of them were swollen and tender. One a bit more than the other.

Shadow had always been a good horse, but was going on sixteen years of age. And he'd never pulled a wagon before. Or a shell of a Ford pickup either, for that matter.

Sal was certain it was equine arthritis.

And that meant two things. First, it wasn't just some passing ailment that would get better on its own. And second, it would be cruel to continue putting the horse through more abuse.

He found a nice place to camp for a few days at a state park west of Kansas City. Found a four-man tent in the back of a trailer bound for a sporting goods store in Phoenix. Figured nobody would miss it.

He also took two hundred feet of nylon rope from the same truck and unhooked the horses.

Sal was a horseman all his life. He thought it cruel to hobble a horse, yet couldn't trust them to free graze without wandering off. If they wandered out of his view they'd probably be stolen. And that would present an even bigger problem than the one he already had.

He took the rope and looped it once around a sturdy oak tree, then tied each end of the rope to the horses' leads. When Shadow allowed some slack in the rope, Max could walk farther from the tree. When Max allowed some slack Shadow could do likewise. However, both were still tethered to the tree and couldn't go far. The grass hadn't been mowed in over a year and was knee high. And the tree was only fifty feet or so from a playa lake.

It was time to relax and rest. Humans and equines alike.

## Chapter 5

On the second day in camp, Sal managed to shoot a rabbit from sixty yards away. It was a lucky shot, as Sal's eyesight was failing and he wasn't a great shot even in his younger years.

Sal's shot would have gone cleanly by the left side of the rabbit, except the creature spooked as Sal was pulling the trigger. The sad fact of the matter was, the rabbit ran into the bullet rather than the other way around.

But Sal didn't care. The result was the same. And he and Nellie had fresh meat for the first time in two weeks.

On the third day Sal finally realized there were fish in the playa lake. He was a much better fisherman than he was a hunter. He filled his stringer twice that day, and twice again the next day.

It was far more than he needed and he could have left some in the water for others who'd come later. But old Sal just couldn't help himself. And he didn't know when he'd find another place so chock full. Or the time to fish.

So he took way more than he should have. He and Nellie had their fill and he turned the rest into fish jerky. They'd be snacking on it for many miles to come.

On the evening of the fifth day he reexamined Shadow's leg. The swelling had gone down, but not appreciably so. The strain on the joint wasn't from hauling the pickup. It was arthritis, brought on by advancing age.

And pulling the pickup certainly didn't help.

Shadow still walked with a slight limp as he hooked up his team. He needed to be put out to pasture. But for the time being there was no alternative. Asking Max to pull the rig by himself would only cause him injury as well.

Sal patted Shadow's shoulder and said, "Just a little bit longer, boy. We'll find somebody to replace you and let you live out your remaining years munching on grass and crapping in a field somewhere."

Sal took the rig off the interstate and started traveling the country roads, stopping frequently to ask residents whether they knew of any horses for sale. By now he had a zippered money bag full of gold rings, bracelets and chains. Plenty, he figured, to pay for a sturdy horse.

And that was how he and Nellie had come upon Karen and Tommy's farm house not far from Leavenworth, Kansas.

Two of Swain's best men were on the gate that day. Men who knew Swain's drug dealer and would let him in and out without any hassles. And who had enough common sense to pick and choose any number of other visitors who showed up occasionally to visit with Swain or ask him for favors.

"What can we do for you, old man?"

"I've got an old horse that's going lame. I'm looking for someone who has a new horse to sell me. And perhaps willing to take mine as a partial payment."

One of the sentries laughed out loud at Sal.

"Now, why would anyone take your old horse as partial payment when you yourself say it's going lame?"

"Horses are good for more than riding and hauling, my friend."

"You want to sire an old horse? Is he still capable?"

"He is like me, my friend. He doesn't feel romantic as often as he once did. But occasionally he is in the mood and is certainly capable."

The sentry laughed once more. But he thought Swain might get a kick out of seeing the skeleton of a pickup truck being drawn by two horses.

"Okay, old man. Come on in," he said as stepped to one side. "Drive on up to the house. Tell the man on the porch you're here to see Mr. Swain."

Sal repeated the name so he wouldn't forget it.

"Mr. Swain. Very well. Thank you, sir."

Sal slowly drove the team up a long caliche drive toward the farm house. There were several children playing in the yard out front. Ring Around the Rosie. They appeared to be having a joyous time.

All activity stopped, though, once the rig got close enough for the children to hear the clop, clop, clop of the horses' hooves.

All heads turned. Jaws dropped. Giggles were heard.

None of the children, or those adults present either for that matter, had ever seen two horses pulling a pickup truck before.

The man on the porch, a rifle cradled in his hands at the ready, walked down the steps to greet him.

"Hello, stranger. State your business."

"The men at the gate told me I could talk to a man named Swain. I'm interested in buying one of his horses."

The guard smiled. Not because he didn't believe the man on the rig. But because he knew for a fact Swain had no horses to sell. He had only a few for the mounted patrols, and had always stated publicly that he wanted more.

Perhaps the men on the gate thought the man was an easy mark, and let him in to be swindled or robbed.

"Mr. Swain is napping. Would you like to talk to his assistant?"

"Yes sir. That would be fine."

The man went back to the door and knocked on it. Someone opened it up and he whispered something old Sal could not hear. Then he went back to his original position adjacent to the door, rifle at the ready, in case he was needed further.

Ruben Sanchez walked out the door, obviously a bit irritated at being disturbed.

He couldn't help but smile, though, at the sight of the pickup-turned-wagon.

He walked down the steps trying not to chuckle. At least until he found out what the old man wanted.

Sal stepped off the rig and reached out his hand.

Sanchez ignored it and started to walk around the pickup, with Sal in tow. Sanchez smiled broadly, no longer hiding his disdain at the Ford Ranger.

"You make this yourself, old man?"

"Yes, I did."

"Ain't much to look at, is it now?"

"I wasn't aiming for beauty, my friend. I was aiming for something to get me where I wanted to go."

Sanchez paused to formulate a good response when both men were distracted.

Nellie had opened the pickup's door and was stepping out. She was looking into the distance and muttering something.

They were her first words in several days.

She said, "Becky! Thank God we've found you!"

## Chapter 6

Nellie had been hallucinating for days. In her fragile mind, she and Sal were still on their way to Vito's house.

In her mind, they never arrived at the house and found the bodies. Never buried them. Never prayed over them.

She'd blacked it all out.

In her mind, Vito and Melissa and Becky were alive and well and waiting for them.

In her mind, the little girl playing in the yard with the raven hair and ponytail, who bore a striking resemblance to Becky, was Becky herself.

She stepped out of the pickup and ran to the child.

Several things all happened at once.

The man on the porch, sensing a threat but not understanding what it might be, lifted his rifle and followed Nellie across the yard with it.

Nellie broke into tears as she neared the young child.

Little Beth Spears, confused by the woman running toward her and calling her a strange name, shied away.

Sanchez, as confused as everyone else, started to mutter, "What the…"

Sal, seeing the man with the rifle aimed at his wife, yelled, "Don't shoot!"

The man didn't shoot. But it wasn't because Sal told him not to. He just happened to be one of the few men in Swain's employ who would not shoot an unarmed elderly woman in the back.

Sanchez and Sal watched from a distance as Nellie reached the young girl in the yard and swept her up into her arms.

Sanchez turned to Sal and demanded, "What in the hell is going on, old man?"

"Please. My wife is ill. That girl looks like the granddaughter we buried a few weeks ago. Our only granddaughter. The only one we can ever have. She hasn't been right in the head ever since. Please forgive us. I think she believes that girl is our Becky."

Sanchez was confused. And more than a little bit angry. For although he certainly felt no attachment to the girl in the yard, he hated being blindsided. Or put into a situation where he lost control of things. And when Swain was sleeping he was in charge. Somebody driving a wagon into the yard and chasing after one of his hostages made him look bad.

More than anything else, Ruben Sanchez hated it when he looked bad.

Still, he tried to control his anger.

"Exactly what is it you want, old man?"

"I am sorry for my wife's behavior. We simply came here to buy a horse. One of ours is going lame, you see, and needs to be put out to pasture."

"You have money to pay for such a horse?"

"Yes, sir. We have some gold."

"How much are you willing to pay?"

"That would depend on the horse."

Sanchez was tempted to just shoot the old man and his stupid wife, take their ridiculous rig, and all the gold they had on them.

But that would have created a couple of problems.

First, Swain had gone upstairs to sleep.

But Sanchez knew something about Swain that many of his men did not know.

Swain was a dope addict. Methamphetamines. He very seldom slept. The speed kept him awake for five, six nights at a time. In all likelihood he was up in his room in a drug-induced stupor. Gunshots would have disturbed him and interrupted his high. Swain hated to be interrupted when he was getting high. It made him grumpy and ready to pounce and yell at somebody.

Sanchez hated getting yelled at.

Second, Swain hated it when things went on without his knowledge. He was a micromanager. He was not going to allow a horse to be sold without his direct knowledge and consent. And he was always bitching about needing more horses, so he probably wouldn't agree to the sale even if asked.

Third, Swain hated clutter. And litter. At the sound of gunshots he'd come charging outside in a very foul mood, throwing a tantrum like a child and demanding to know who in hell shot who and why. Then he'd see the ridiculous rig in the center of the yard and brand it ugly and an eyesore.

He'd say it made his kingdom look cluttered and order Sanchez to get rid of it.

And Sanchez didn't want the damn thing either.

The old man was looking at Sanchez while Sanchez was trying to decide what to do. He didn't know that Sanchez was contemplating his fate.

Then Sanchez had an idea. An absolutely great idea.

"I'm sorry, old man. We have no horses to sell. But we can discuss making a deal for the little girl if your wife fancies her so."

Sal was taken aback.

"Excuse me?"

Ruben Sanchez wasn't the brightest guy around. In fact, he was good at very few things. One was killing. Another was lying. He could spin a yarn as well as any man, and think on his feet.

"We are an orphanage. We take in all the orphaned children in the area. Those children whose parents died in the plague, or killed themselves. Or fell victim to somebody else's gun. If your wife fancies the girl, and believes it to be her own, perhaps we should pacify her and send the girl with you."

Sal was stunned. He truly didn't know what to say.

So Sanchez continued to spin his tale.

"Since the power is out, we are unable to contact the state of Kansas. Therefore we are forced to operate on our own. An independent adoption agency, if you will. So there is no formal paperwork to fill out or waiting period, or even an approval process. You simply promise to provide a good home for the child, pay an adoption fee, and take possession."

The words "take possession" had an eerie ring to them. As though a child were nothing more than a used car.

Sal looked across the yard. Nellie was on one knee, the young girl standing in front of her. Nellie was holding both the girl's hands and conversing with her. The smile on Nellie's face was the first Sal had seen in a very long time.

He turned to Sanchez and asked, "How much, sir, is the adoption fee?"

## Chapter 7

Sanchez choked at the question and had a very difficult time stifling a laugh.

But he quickly composed himself.

After all, there was money on the line.

"Seven pieces of silver."

It was, from his perspective, a totally random number.

And one he totally expected to be dismissed outright.

For he had no clue what adoption agencies or the states which oversaw them charged for processing fees.

Nor was Sanchez a student of the Bible, for he was a man who didn't believe in God.

If he had been, surely he'd have seen the irony of suggesting that seven pieces of silver was the going rate for doing the deplorable.

For his part, old Sal thought the price was a bit high.

But he was bordering on desperate. His wife would surely not let him leave without her precious grandchild.

And Sal held absolutely none of the cards.

So he pounced on the offer before it was withdrawn. And perhaps rose to a higher figure.

"Done," he said while offering his hand.

Sanchez shook the hand. He had to, for in his band a welsh was as bad as a snitch.

But even as he was shaking Sal's hand he was wishing he'd asked for twenty silver pieces instead of only seven.

Still, he'd have seven pieces of silver in his pocket that he didn't have when he woke up that morning. That in itself made it a pretty good day.

Sanchez took the seven Morgan dollars Sal fished out of a pocket, all the time fighting the urge to just shoot the couple and take whatever else they had.

But had he done so, he'd have still been stuck with little Beth.

Sanchez didn't like her much, you see. She had a mouth on her. Little Beth was always demanding that Swain and his band of thugs go away and leave them alone. She especially didn't like that Swain was constantly taking her mom into his bedroom for hours at a time. And that Swain was particularly brutal to all the children when her mom wasn't around.

She even kicked Sanchez in the ankle one day when he told her to get her snotty little ass in the house and do some housework.

He'd let the old man live, and the old woman too. They'd take the snotty kid with them, and he'd have a pocket full of silver to boot.

It wouldn't be the worst of days, by any means.

"Let me go talk to her for a minute," he told Sal. "Alone. I need to explain to her what we're doing, so she won't try to run away from you."

Sal understood. It was important, he imagined, that the child be assured by someone she knew and trusted that she wasn't going to be harmed in any way. That this couple would accept her and love her and treat her well.

"I understand," Sal said. "I'll get Nellie away from her for a few minutes and explain to her that you've been taking good care of Becky, and that she'll be coming with us now."

Nellie didn't want to leave the child's side, of course. Sal had to coax her away a little at a time. Even when they were separated by forty feet, Nellie's eyes remained locked on the girl, her hands outstretched in Beth's direction.

Sanchez went to Beth and took a knee. He wanted to convey to the old couple that he was a compassionate friend of the child, when in reality he was anything but.

Beth crossed her arms in a defiant posture and demanded of Sanchez, "Just what in the world is going on?"

"Shhh. Not so loud."

He started spinning a great tale. One which wouldn't have impressed an adult with even a hint of common sense. But which might make perfect sense to a snot of a seven year old girl going on eight.

"I want you to go with these people to get some medicine for your Aunt Karen."

"What do you mean?"

"Your mom didn't tell you?"

"Tell me what?"

"Your aunt has a sickness. A sickness that can only be cured with penicillin. Do you know what penicillin is?"

"I've heard Mommy and Daddy talk about it."

"So you know it's a medicine?"

"I guess so."

"Atta girl. Well, it's very hard to find, but these people know where some is. They're going to get it and bring it back here so they can use it to save your Aunt Karen's life. You want to help save your Aunt Karen's life, don't you?"

"She doesn't look sick."

"Oh, but she is. She's been trying to hide it from you kids so she doesn't worry you. But she's very sick and without the penicillin she'll die very soon. You don't want your Mommy's sister to die, do you? Think how sad your Mommy will be."

"Why do I have to go with them? Why can't they go get it and bring it back on their own?"

"Because the old man can't see very well. He can't read the road signs. He needs someone to help read the road signs so he doesn't get lost. You can read road signs, can't you?"

Beth suddenly grew defiant.

"Of course I can! I'm not stupid, you know."

Then, in a wary tone, "How come the woman can't read the signs for him?"

"Because she's sick as well. In her mind. That's why she calls you Becky, because she's confused.

"Will the penicillin help her too?"

"Why, yes. Yes it will. It'll make her all better too."

"I think I should check with my Mommy first."

"You can't. Swain just took your Mommy up to his room. She'll be up there for hours. And you know how mean Swain gets when he's interrupted. He might get angry and beat your mother. You wouldn't want that, would you?"

Sanchez knew Beth would find this part of his tale particularly plausible. For she'd seen Swain beat her mother on several occasions in the past.

"Here's the thing," Sanchez continued. "If you don't go with them right now to get the medicine, it'll be too late. Your Aunt Karen will die and your mother will have a broken heart. You can help, but you must go now."

Beth was wavering. She didn't trust Sanchez. Not at all. But she loved her mother and her aunt and didn't want to see pain nor harm come to either of them.

"How long will we be gone?"

"Just three or four days. And the old people will take very good care of you, I promise."

"Well, okay. And you'll tell my Mommy where I went?"

"I certainly will. I promise."

## Chapter 8

Beth climbed into the cab of the Ford Ranger, her little heart and mind telling her she was doing something kind to help those she loved the most.

Sanchez took old Sal aside.

"She has a lot of good friends here. She doesn't want to go. I hate to say it, but I had to mislead her. It's the only way I could convince her to go with you."

"Deceive her how?"

"I told her you were going to find penicillin for her sick auntie. And that you'd return in a few days."

Sal was aghast.

"But what will she do when she finds out you've lied to her?"

"She won't do anything. Just avoid her questions. And then when you're three or four days away, tell her she misunderstood me. That you never said you were going for medicine. That we decided to send her someplace safer. When you're several days away, she won't have any choice but to stay with you. She won't run away because she's a smart girl. She'll know she could never find her way back."

"We're headed to Albuquerque. If she ran away she'd die in the desert."

"Then tell her that. But wait until you're well on your way. Let her believe you'll be bringing her back, until you're too far away for her to walk back."

Sal was a good man. A bit gruff on the exterior sometimes, but a decent and kind and giving man. And he was honest as well. He hated deceiving anyone.

Especially a child.

But when he looked into Nellie's eyes he could see the pure love and joy she had for the child she believed to be her granddaughter.

Becky had been taken from her once.

Sal didn't have the heart to allow her to be taken a second time.

Sal tried to rationalize the problem. To tell himself that what he was doing wasn't right. But that perhaps it was best for the girl in the long run.

After all, the man at the orphanage said she'd lost her family.

And wouldn't it be better for her in the long run to give her another family? An older couple who'd love her and care for her and guide her?

An orphanage was no place for a child to be raised.

Not when Sal and Nellie were willing to take her in.

It went against his grain as a decent man.

But he'd do what the man at the orphanage suggested.

He'd be vague with his answers. He'd lead the girl to believe she was going on a mercy run. A run to find and procure medication for her sick aunt.

Eventually he'd have to tell her the truth. But he'd wait until they were very far away.

He'd take her by the hand and explain that she was misled, sure. But it was for her own good.

"You'll see," he'd tell her. "We'll treat you like our very own granddaughter. We'll be kind and will protect you. You're much better off with us than you would have been at that orphanage."

Eventually Sal would have that conversation with the child. Just the two of them, while Nellie slept.

And then he'd learn that the "orphanage" wasn't an orphanage at all. It was an armed camp, run by hostile men. And that Sal and Nellie were lucky to be allowed to leave with their lives.

And the small girl.

Eventually Sal would be faced with a dreadful decision.

For the humane thing to do would be to take the girl back. To reunite her with her mother and sister.

But while that might be the most humane course of action for the girl and the proper thing to do, it would destroy Nellie.

And Nellie had made so much progress in recent days.

In the end, he decided he owed his allegiance to Nellie. He insisted to the girl that she was legally adopted. That it was much too late to go back and change anything.

And that her new name was Becky.

And each night, as he lay down to sleep, his decision haunted him.

## Chapter 9

It took another week to solve the problem with Shadow's bad knees.

He got slower and slower as each day went by. The ground they covered each day got shorter and shorter.

And what made it worse was the burden the other horse, Max, had to carry. As he accepted more and more than his share of the load, he started showing more signs of stress himself.

They'd stopped at every ranch and farm along the way until they finally came to one which had a sturdy horse grazing in the yard.

The Peters family was in dire straits.

They'd lost two able-bodied sons to marauders. The mother was wheelchair bound. The father had a bad heart. They were both in their seventies.

It was just a matter of time.

They depended solely on a third son, Spencer.

Spencer was a good man, a fearless man. That he reminded most strangers more of Forrest Gump than Albert Einstein was irrelevant. For no one really expected him to solve complex equations or the mysteries of the universe.

Not often, anyway.

If he was deemed a bit on the slow side it didn't really matter, for there was nothing adherently difficult about running the small farm on which he lived with his aged parents.

It was a lot of work for one man. But he was strong and he could handle it.

Still, they were struggling, through no fault of Spencer's.

When Spencer's brothers were murdered he had no clue how to gather food from the trucks on the highway. They had sheltered him from that part of the operation, figuring he was safer back at the farm with their mom and dad.

They certainly did him no favors. But then again, they weren't expecting to be ambushed and shot in the back for the guns they were toting.

Spencer was able to find a few trucks, but they'd mostly been emptied of anything worth taking. There were more trucks farther out, but he didn't want to venture too far.

He was easily confused, you see, and was prone to forgetting which direction he came from and which he was going.

He was, as the term implied, directionally challenged.

So his mother and father told him to stay at home.

They lived on a farm, after all. They could grow what they needed, and drink from the well.

Then the drought came.

Almost four long months came and went without a drop of rain.

Spencer did what he could to irrigate a limited amount of corn and wheat.

But the pump house no longer worked.

The windmill pumped enough water to fill the stock tanks. But when Spencer used most of it to irrigate the crops, the cattle started dropping like flies.

Spencer lacked the mental capacity to realize he could keep a few head of cattle alive, and a few rows of crops, but no better than that.

Instead, he tried to save everything, and in the process lost almost all of it.

The last three head of beef fell dead not from thirst, but from some kind of disease.

It was the final straw.

The three of them... mom, dad, and simpleton son, fell into a general funk together. They more or less gave up and waited to die.

Then old Sal and Nellie stumbled onto their farm in a red Ranger pickup truck drawn by two horses.

One broken down and the other wasn't far behind.

Spencer met him in the yard.

"Whadda y'all want?"

It wasn't that Spencer was trying to be rude, necessarily. It was just that he no longer trusted strangers.

"I saw your horse from the roadway," Sal explained. "One of ours is going lame. He needs to be put out to pasture. I wonder if you'd be willing to take him as partial trade and sell your horse to us."

"Sell him for how much?"

"I'll give you two ounces of gold, and our lame horse in trade."

"Hold on, mister. Lemme go ask my Daddy."

While he waited, Sal dismounted and took it upon himself to examine the pony grazing in the front yard. A Paint, maybe five years old and sturdy. He came from good stock.

Spencer appeared on the front porch again.

"Daddy wants to know what two ounces of gold is worth."

Sal yelled back, "About eight hundred dollars, more or less."

He really didn't have a clue, but it sounded reasonable to him.

Spencer came out much quicker the second time, and met Sal in the yard.

"Daddy says you got yourself a deal, so long as you got the gold on ya. He says we don't want no IOU."

Sal had no scale with which to weigh the gold. But he erred on the heavy side, and probably gave away closer to three ounces than two.

But that was okay. He was desperate to replace Shadow before both horses went lame. And now that he knew where to look for it, he knew he could replace the gold in a few days by looking through the trucks as he came across them.

"Now, old Shadow has been through a lot," he explained to Spencer as he unhooked the old horse from the rig. "Promise me you'll give him a long life. Let him live out his days grazing on long grass in a peaceful meadow, instead of making him work any more."

"Oh heck, I reckon so," Spencer agreed.

The new Paint seemed to take well to the rig. He'd obviously towed heavy wagons before and was strong and capable.

Old Sal was supremely happy.

So happy that as he left the farmhouse and got back onto the highway, he barely heard the rifle shot in the distance.

And even if he'd heard it, he'd have paid it no mind.

For there wouldn't have been any reason at all to associate it with the man he'd just left.

Or with old Shadow, who'd seen his last sunrise and who now lay dead in the rich red Oklahoma dirt.

Sal had no way of knowing that Spencer's father had given him instructions that morning to dispatch the Paint. To send his soul to the big horse ranch in the sky.

They were desperate for fresh meat, as it turned out.

And while nobody would admit to favoring horse meat over beef, it worked in a pinch.

The flesh from a full-grown horse would provide them steaks for several days and jerky for several months.

It turned out that Sal's visit and offer were godsends to them. They were planning on butchering a horse before the day was out anyway.

Didn't matter much to them which horse it was.

The gold would help them a lot in buying enough provisions to get them by for a few weeks. Hopefully until God blessed them with a heavy rainstorm or two.

But it wouldn't fill their bellies in the short term.

Sal's old horse would do that.

And if Spencer had to break his promise to Sal to spare the horse and let him retire peacefully in a meadow?

Well, that was too darned bad, as Spencer would say.

He owed his allegiance to his maw and paw. Not to some broken down old man in a funny-looking pickup truck.

## Chapter 10

*Present Day...*

Dave Speer still wasn't sure how far he trusted Tony.

Despite Tony's calm demeanor, and the fact he looked more like an accountant than a drug dealer, he was a purveyor of a very dangerous product in a very dangerous world.

They were an odd couple if there ever was one. A family man, a former Marine who was as patriotic and law-abiding as any American could ever be.

Teamed up with a drug dealer who dealt unscrupulous people their choice of poisons, without regard to where they got the money to pay for them.

Of course, to hear Tony tell it, he was doing society a big favor.

"You have to cut these people a break," he tried to explain to Dave. "They've been through hell. Something *ten times* worse than hell. If they feel a need to escape reality to help themselves cope with this new dangerous and chaotic world, then who are you or I to judge?"

Dave wasn't buying it.

"But you know you're destroying their minds. You're doing them no favors."

"That's where you're wrong, my new and slightly naïve friend.

"I give them a quality product. One I'd have no hesitation in using myself if I were so inclined. The stuff I sell to them isn't cut with Draino or crushed salt or talcum powder. It's as pure as snow, if you'll pardon the pun. That's because I only do business with people I can trust.

"And my buyers, in turn, trust me. They know I'm picky about who my suppliers are. They know I won't buy from just anybody. They know that when they pump that shit into their arm or suck it into their lungs that they'll get high instead of die. *That's* how I'm helping them.

"I didn't put that monkey on their back. It was there long before I came along. But since it's there and I know how vicious it can be, I'm helping them to deal with the monkey safely until they decide to kick the habit. When they tell me they're tired of the monkey and ready to quit, I help them."

"Yeah, right. A drug dealer with a conscience. A drug dealer who helps his customers get off the shit."

"It's true. Ask around."

Dave did ask around. And he found out it was indeed true. Some of the cleanest people in the camps east and north of Albuquerque; some of Tony's closest friends, were once Tony's customers.

"Here's the bottom line, Dave. When these people are in the shit and haven't yet decided to get clean, they're gonna get it from somewhere. If they get it from me at least it'll be clean. If they get it from somewhere else, there's a fifty percent chance or better it'll be cut. Sometimes with stuff that won't hurt them.

"And sometimes with stuff that can kill them."

In the end they were at an impasse. Tony didn't convince Dave he was a drug dealer with morals; a man who was into helping his customers get off the junk when they wanted to instead of hooking them forever.

But Dave couldn't fight the feeling that he liked the man, drug dealer or not.

And that was good. Because for better or worse, they were partners.

And partners worked best together when they didn't hate one another.

"So, where are we going first?" Dave asked from the passenger seat of Tony's Polaris as they navigated around the abandoned cars and trucks on the interstate.

"This part of town belongs to the Crips. Their turf is everything south of I-40 and east of I-25. Probably eighty square miles or so."

"That's a big chunk."

"It is. It was split between them and a group called Sanders' Freedom Fighters, but they just finished a turf war and sent the Sanders group packing. Killed about half of them."

"The Sanders' Freedom Fighters, huh? What kind of freedoms were they fighting for?"

"Mostly their own personal freedom to rape, rob and plunder. They were bad, but not the worst. I won't miss them much."

"Are the Crips any better?"

"Not generally. But at least their leadership is more stable."

## Chapter 11

It was eerily quiet as the Polaris made its way along Interstate 40.

Tony drove in the eastbound lanes, dodging abandoned cars and trucks which were facing toward them.

Dave's curiosity finally got the best of him.

"Not that it really matters anymore, but why are you driving against traffic?"

"You haven't noticed the cars?"

"Which cars? The ones all over the place with their headlights pointing in our direction?"

"No. The cars that are blocking all the on-ramps and exits."

It turned out that Dave had noticed. He just never said anything.

On every on-ramp, at the point where it connected with the freeway, an abandoned car had been pushed across the ramp to effectively block it.

And across both sides of the car, in fluorescent blue spray paint, was the single world "CRIPS."

Across every exit ramp was another car painted exactly the same way.

"Look on the other side of the highway," Tony said. "The exits and ramps are marked the same way, except the cars are painted "LOS LOBOS."

"I saw that," Dave said. "And I know who the Crips are. Who are Los Lobos?"

"Los Lobos is Spanish for the wolves. They were an Albuquerque street gang before the blackout. Absolutely brutal. One of the worst. They were the first ones to stake out their territory and begin kicking out non-gang members. They went door to door a week after the blackout and handed each resident an eviction notice."

"Seriously?"

"Yes. They had them made up in Spanish first, then English. It said the residents had seven days to vacate the premises. After seven days they'd return and kill one family member. And then they'd return every seven days until they were all dead or gone. It was pretty effective."

"They didn't go to the cops?"

"There was no way to get to the cops, except for walking. And anybody who left the neighborhoods on foot was questioned about where they were going. The rumor I heard was that one guy made it downtown by traveling at night. The cops told him he was on his own. The cops were deserting right and left and staying home to protect their own families. Many of them read the writing on the wall and were getting their families out of the city while they still could.

"The story goes that the guy who went to the cops was the very first man in Albuquerque to get his head on a stick."

"His head on a stick?"

"Yes. Besides the painted cars, it's one of the main ways the gangs mark their territories. They kill their enemies, and sometimes regular citizens who didn't leave town soon enough. They put their heads on a stick and paint them in their gang colors.

"The Los Lobos use red. If you come to a street that has a red-painted severed head on a stick, stuck into the ground on the corner, that street belongs to Los Lobos. You'd better stay the hell off of it unless you're a member of the gang or affiliated with them in some way.

"Or, if you're like us and get safe passage because you have guns or drugs or something else they want."

"Does it ever make you nervous, coming in here knowing that they could turn on you in a heartbeat?"

"Of course it does. Not as much as it used to. They've learned that I offer the best shit available, that it's high quality and uncut.

"They also know that I never reveal my sources. Not to anyone. Not even to you.

"That's not because I'm necessarily secretive. It's for my own protection. Because as long as my sources are known only to me, they'll keep me alive. If I were to die, that information would die with me. And then they'd have to deal with everybody else. Half the dope they bought would be cut, and most of the rest of it would be crap. And some of it would be downright dangerous."

At mile marker 164 the pair drove the wrong way down an on-ramp around a 1977 Cadillac Deville decorated with Crip colors.

Dave remarked, "It must have taken a lot of time, pushing all these cars onto the ramps and then painting them all."

"True. But then, there's not an awful lot of stuff to do anymore without electricity. They've got a lot of time to kill these days."

Tony pulled up to what struck Dave as some kind of checkpoint.

It was a Class C recreational vehicle, an upscale Winnebago, sitting diagonally smack dab in the middle of an intersection.

Milling about were half a dozen gang members, dressed mostly in blue.

And heavily armed.

"Who the hell's this?" one of them asked Tony while nodding in Dave's direction.

"His name's Dave. He's my new partner. Dave, this is Tiny, Blue and Bobo."

No one offered any greeting or handshakes. It was apparently beneath them. They were on their own turf and felt no real need to be either hospitable or friendly.

Dave nodded in their direction, not as an indication of subservience, but rather merely to acknowledge their existence.

"Daaaamn, Tony. Drug sales must be pretty damn good for you to be needin' a damn partner all of a sudden."

"Sales *are* good, Bobo. Real good. But he won't be doing my drugs. We're branchin' out. He's gonna be haulin' hooch."

"Now you're talkin'. Now *that's* some feel good I can get into my own self. When's he gonna start runnin'?"

"Probably in a few days. We're working on the details now. I want to introduce him to Hell Boi, find out what he needs and how much, so we can hook him up."

Bobo addressed Dave directly for the first time. It was as though he just then noticed him.

"You bring in the good shit, now, you hear? None of that cheap shit. And find a good stash of Crystal for me. I drink a lot of that shit, but it's gettin' pretty damn hard to find 'round here lately."

"I already got a handle on it, my friend. I'll bring you a couple of bottles on the house, next time I come in."

"All right, *now* we talkin.'"

Bobo turned back to Tony and said "Hell Boi at the house. You know where it's at."

"Yes, I do. Later, fellas."

As they drove down the street, Tony leaned over to Dave and said, "Well congratulations. You passed the first test and did well."

"Because I made some new friends?"

"No. Because you didn't get us both killed."

## Chapter 13

"Who the hell is he?"

The question, which Dave expected to hear over and over again in coming days, came from a tall, thin black man. He reminded Dave of a character named Huggy Bear in an old 1970s crime drama Dave had forgotten the name of.

The man followed up the question with an observation:

"Man, you know I don't trust white people."

Tony countered, "I'm a white people."

"You're different, man."

"How so?"

"You got somethin' I want. You're a white people I tolerate."

"You'll tolerate him too. He's my new partner. His name is Dave. He's gonna start runnin' booze for me."

"What kind of booze?"

"Whatever you need, bro. Colt 44, Ripple. Whatever you need."

"Man, that's racist, you cracker."

"So's cracker, you big dummy."

Hell Boi turned to Dave and did something Dave totally didn't expect.

He held out his hand for a handshake.

Not the old man handshake of Dave's father's generation, the kind two old friends give to each other at church on Sundays. No, this was a bro handshake. A cool shake.

A handshake that told Dave that while his skin was lighter than Hell Boi would have preferred, he was accepted.

That he and Hell Boi might never be friends. But they'd be able to do business.

"When you gonna start runnin' your hooch, man?"

"That's just it. I've got the merchandize. I still need a way to move it. We've heard about a red pickup truck movin' somewhere around Albuquerque. It no longer has an engine. Instead, it's being pulled by two horses. An old couple is riding around in it. We want to find it. It'll be perfect for driving my merchandize around the city."

"You gonna sell your stuff to the other factions too?"

Tony answered for Dave: "Hell yeah, dude. We're businessmen. We'll sell to anybody who gots the gold. You know how it is."

Hell Boi wasn't pleased, but he did indeed know how it worked.

"Okay. Just promise you'll stop here first. Give me first crack at what you got."

"You have my word, man."

The tall man seemed satisfied.

"So," Tony continued. "We need some help finding that red pickup truck. You seen it?"

"Me personally, no. Somethin' like that I'd definitely remember. Let me ask my lieutenants."

He turned and whispered something to an aide, or more likely a bodyguard, standing silently behind him.

The man disappeared into another room.

Dave got an uneasy feeling, but it was unfounded. The man reappeared with three other men, all of who were unarmed. They'd have been loaded for bear if there was any trouble amiss.

Hell Boi addressed the newcomers.

"These crackers are looking for a red pickup truck, pulled by two horses. Driven by two old people. You guys seen anything like that?"

The three looked at each other, shook their heads and shrugged their shoulders.

One of them uttered the now predictable, "No, man. If I saw somethin' like that I damn sure woulda remembered it."

"So you're sure there's nothin' like that anywhere on our turf?"

"Oh, hell no. Shit, if I saw somethin' like that I'd probably shoot the old folks and take it for my own self."

Dave winced at the words, then hoped nobody noticed.

Hell Boi offered, "Maybe you got ahead of 'em. Maybe they just ain't here yet."

Tony said, "Maybe. Would you watch out for them for us?"

"No problem, man. We'll shoot those old mothers off the damn thing and save it for you when you come back again."

"No, please don't do that," Dave blurted out.

The others looked at him, not sure what to make of his words.

He'd stepped in it and he knew it. If they suspected there was another reason he wanted the wagon, there was a good chance they'd find it, and Beth, and demand a ransom to get her back.

Tony sensed his story would be more believable than Dave's and stepped in to help.

"The old folks, they're traveling with a little girl. Dave had three girls and they all got shot a few months ago. He has a soft spot for kids and don't want any shootin' because he don't want the girl to get hurt. He'd rather just find the old people and buy the pickup from them instead."

"I got a girl my own self," Hell Boi said. "I ain't seen her in three years now. I don't even know where the hell she at. I feel ya."

The fire put out, Dave breathed a sigh of relief. He'd have to be more careful in the future.

He exchanged glances with Tony. Tony's eyes told him the same thing.

Hell Boi turned to his lieutenants.

"Tell the fellas to watch out for them. A red pickup truck with two horses and some old people. Tell them to stop them, but not to hurt them. Bring them here to see me."

He turned back to Tony.

"How soon you coming back?"

"Three days. Can you hold them here that long?"

"No problem, my lily-white assed cracker friend. We'll treat 'em like family."

"Good."

"Now then, down to business. You got my usual shit?"

Tony dug into his bag and Dave got the feeling he'd passed the first of many tests.

# Chapter 14

"How close was that bullet we dodged?" Dave asked when he and Tony were back on the road.

"Don't beat yourself up over it. It wasn't that bad. Every man, even the bad ones, has a soft spot for little kids. Nobody wants to see little kids get hurt. It was an unfortunate comment, but you recovered nicely."

"Yeah. By letting you do the talking."

"Let's look upon that as an opportunity to learn, Dave. From now on try to let me do most of the talking."

"Good idea."

They drove on along I-40 until it intersected with I-25, then headed south.

"It's not true."

Dave's cryptic comment caught Tony off guard.

"What? What's not true?"

"Not all men have a soft spot for little kids. Not all of them hate the thought of little kids getting hurt or killed."

Tony turned to look at him.

He almost asked, but thought better of it. He could plainly see in Dave's eyes that Dave had seen things... horrific things, that men had done to children since the lights went out.

And Tony decided he didn't want to hear about them.

One thing Tony would likely never tell Dave was that he had two small children of his own.

Two boys, four and six, who lived with their mother in Smyrna, Georgia.

Two boys he hadn't seen in a very long time.

He and Rachel were on the outs over his chosen profession.

"I don't want our sons to grow up having to visit their father in prison when the cops finally catch up with you," she told him.

He'd countered, "But honey, the money is too damn good to pass up. I can make ten times what I'd make selling insurance or real estate. And I'm careful. Real careful."

"How long are you going to do this, Tony? How long am I going to have to wonder whether this is the day they finally lock you up?"

"Give me six months, honey. You can see I'm saving the money. In six months we'll have enough to buy a house and have a comfortable nest egg. Then I'll quit, I promise."

Tony meant it. He even marked the day on the calendar. On May 10th he'd stop selling drugs forever.

But Rachel didn't want to wait that long.

"I'm taking the boys to my mom's. When you leave this crap behind you, you can come to Smyrna and join us."

Tony had been conflicted. Not only was what he was doing illegal, it was also morally reprehensible.

He knew that.

But those six months would set them up financially for years to come.

In the end, he didn't give in, didn't chase her.

In the end he let them go.

And started marking off each day on his calendar with a big black "X".

Now, he didn't know if his family was dead or alive.

Smyrna was a suburb of Atlanta, which was roughly 1500 long miles due east.

It was a very long way by any means of travel.

If he walked it was four months, minimum.

And Tony had bad feet. They ran in his family.

Taking his Polaris would ease the burden.

But it would also put a big target on his back.

Not a day went by that he didn't struggle with the decision whether to go or to stay.

If he were honest with himself he'd have admitted that it wasn't the trip which scared him.

It was the possibility of traveling all that way to find his children didn't make it.

After all, most of the population didn't.

Tony's memories of his sons were something he'd never tell Dave.

Not because he didn't like Dave, or didn't trust him.

But because Tony never told anyone.

## Chapter 15

The pair exited the freeway by going around a '57 Chevy, white over red.

At one time, it was in immaculate condition.

It still was, other than a thick coating of dust.

And the "MS-13" spray painted across both its sides.

Once upon a time it would have been something akin to blasphemy to spray paint a classic in such a manner. A personal affront to car enthusiasts all over the country.

Car guys would have been pissed. Some would no doubt have resorted to name-calling.

Some might even have resorted to fisticuffs.

But none of them would have messed with MS-13 to get their point across.

"These guys are bad," Tony said. "Real bad. Try to let me do most of the talking."

"Be my guest."

MS-13, as the Crips had, placed sentries at the main entryways to their territory. The sentries recognized Tony as the pair rode up, and didn't raise their weapons or challenge him in any way.

But they didn't look particularly happy to see them, either.

Tony tried being friendly anyway. It was always his first line of defense.

"Yo, dude. Whassup?"

"Who's that?"

"This is my new partner, Dave. Dave, this is Jesse."

Dave nodded politely.

Jesse stared a hole through him.

Then he turned back to Tony.

"You're not bringing this guy into our home, are you?"

"I have to, Jesse. Luis is gonna want to do business with him."

"Luis does business with you."

"Dave will be dealing with different stuff than what I have. Be nice to him. He'll soon be bringing you your tequila."

"Bullshit. There's no more tequila left in Albuquerque. It's been gone for months."

"Exactly. But there's plenty on the trucks outside the city. And I've already laid claim to twenty of them. We've got enough 1800 to knock you on your ass every day for the rest of your life."

"No shit... for real?"

"For real. We just have to figure out how to move it. That's one of the things we need to talk to Luis about."

"Luis ain't gonna be happy with you bringing a bolillo in here."

"Oh, he will once he finds out we can provide him with tequila."

"Maybe. Maybe not. He's been in a pretty bad mood lately."

As he spoke, he swept his hand toward a row of six severed heads atop spikes, driven into the front yard of a house behind him.

The heads were a couple of days old, Dave guessed. They'd turned gray and were covered with flies, but their eyeballs were still more or less intact.

Dave could still make out the look of wide-eyed terror on some of the faces, The men obviously realized they were about to die.

And he couldn't help but notice at least half of them were white.

It wasn't easy. The skin was gray. But the hair was blond in a couple of cases. And red in another.

"What'd they do?"

"They committed a cardinal sin. They pissed Luis off."

Jesse leaned back and laughed like a madman at his joke.

Dave felt a strange need to chuckle himself, although it was more to ease the pit he felt in his stomach than to acknowledge the joke.

He laughed, but his heart wasn't in it.

"You!" Jesse demanded of one of his underlings. "Take these two to see Luis."

The underling jumped aboard his own Polaris, a couple of model years older than Tony's, and led the way without a word.

They traveled down several residential streets which looked like a war zone.

"They gave the residents an opportunity to leave," Tony explained. "If they refused, they burned their houses down. And sometimes, the fires got away from them and burned other houses as well."

The house they pulled up to was rather nondescript. A one-story ranch style home in the middle of the block. Its brick belied its age, as that of a 1970s style.

Dave supposed it was Luis's way of keeping a low profile, thinking rival gangs would look for him in a more affluent neighborhood.

There were snipers on the roof, armed men in the bushes.

Dave felt uneasy.

Tony had forbidden him from coming in armed.

And Dave felt naked without a means of protecting himself.

Still, he faced the fact that even if he were armed, it would be his gun against several others. And while he faced such odds before and walked away, he didn't particularly want to push his luck again.

When they entered the house, both of them were held at gunpoint and patted down.

Dave was nervous. Tony appeared cool as a cucumber.

A troubling thought suddenly popped into Dave's mind.

The thought that Tony might have set him up.

After the introductions were made, the man they called Luis, who appeared to Dave more monster than man, barked his orders.

"I'm not happy you brought him here," he snarled to Tony. "But go ahead and make your rounds. We'll babysit him until you get back."

Tony wasn't rattled.

He addressed Dave directly.

"Relax. They won't hurt you. I'm going to go do some business and I'll be back in a jiffy."

As soon as Tony was out the door Luis nodded to two of his henchmen.

Each stood on one side and held Dave's arms to immobilize him.

For the first time since he'd left Iraq after his second tour, Dave was convinced he was going to die.

## Chapter 16

Luis sat at his desk and interrogated his visitor.

"We have a few minutes to speak in private. I like Tony. He's a good man. But he doesn't know frijoles about security.

"You know what frijoles are?"

"Yes, sir."

"*Sir.* Well, that's a good start. At least you know which of us is in charge. Now, then. Tony said you're looking for a little red pickup. And you came all the way from Texas to get it."

"Yes, sir."

"Well, that presents a dilemma, gringo. You don't mind if I call you gringo, do you?"

"I love being called gringo."

"The dilemma is I don't believe your sorry ass. It just don't make no sense to me that you would pass up all those shiny red pickups in Texas and come all the way here instead. Now, does that make sense to you, gringo?"

"This is a special pickup, my friend. There are plenty of red pickups in Texas. But there are no other pickups like this one."

"What in hell makes this particular pickup so damn special?"

"It has no motor. It's pulled by horses. I figure it'll be perfect for hauling my booze."

"Why don't you use Tony's Polaris?"

"Not big enough. If I'm gonna supply liquor to the whole city I need something that'll carry a lot more than that. Besides, he says he needs it for his own business."

The man continued to eye him suspiciously, despite Dave's best efforts to charm him.

Dave was a social guy by nature. He normally prided himself on being able to get along with anybody. And to get himself out of any sticky situation.

But this guy just wasn't having any of it.

He stood up from behind the desk. Dave could tell he was a big man, even when he was sitting. The broad shoulders and the fact he had to lean forward to place his elbows on the desk told him that much.

It wasn't until he stood, though, that Dave was able to tell he was half the size of Mount Everest. A full six-eight, probably two hundred eighty pounds.

All of it muscle.

The man sprayed spittle as he spoke in more of a growl than anything else.

"I don't like gringos," he snarled. The look on his face when he said the word "gringos" was probably the same face he made when he bit into something very bitter.

"I don't trust them. In my experience, most gringos who just show up and start asking questions are cops. Or snitches trying to lighten their sentence."

Dave struggled a bit, but the men holding his arms had good grips. And the knife at his throat kept him from putting any real effort into it.

"What's the matter, bolillo? You getting a little bit nervous?"

Dave tried to hide his fear. He got the sense that was what the man was looking for.

"In case you haven't heard, my big friend, there are no more cops. They all ran away like cowards, or died and went straight to hell where they belonged. And I'm exactly what Tony said I was. Just a guy trying to make a buck by hauling liquor for him."

"Then why you asking so many damn questions, gringo?"

"I just like to know who I'm dealing with. If I'm going to be drinking tequila with you, playing cards with you, sharing women with you, I want to know you're a good hombre. As for the horse drawn pickup I'm looking for, I talked to someone who said it was headed for Albuquerque. I can use it to bring your tequila. That's all, my friend."

"You want to be my friend, gringo? Or are you just trying to save your ass, so you don't find out what I did with the last guy who came in here asking questions?"

Dave fell silent. He suspected the man was fishing, but didn't want to take his bait.

"Well, gringo? Aren't you just a little bit curious about what I did to the last curious gato who came through that door?"

"I'm guessing you didn't light up a joint and cook him a steak dinner?"

The man laughed, and Dave thought he was making headway.

Then he stopped laughing, placed his face inches from Dave's and yelled at him.

"I cut off his head and hung it on my wall. We made a dartboard out of it until it started to stink. The eyes were the bull's-eyes. Fifty points apiece. It was a lot of fun, until it started to rot."

He turned his head from side to side, talking to the henchmen who held Dave in place.

"What about it, boys? You up for a few more games of darts?"

Dave wished that Tony would hurry back from wherever the heck he went. And he was really starting to wonder whether Tony sold him out.

He was starting to feel fear, and he didn't like the feeling.

That was Luis's intention, of course. And he was starting to make progress.

Dave would never show it. But he was now certain he'd made a serious error in judgment.

His options were limited. He had no real choice but to try to talk his way out of the situation.

"You know, Luis…. Can I call you Luis?"

The big man laughed.

"Sure. I'm feeling very generous today. You can call me Luis."

"You know, Luis, the game of darts is more about luck than skill. A blind man can hit the bull's-eye if you give him enough throws and point him in the right general direction.

"Poker, on the other hand... now that's a game of great skill, where only the best and smartest survive."

## Chapter 17

It hadn't escaped Dave's attention that Luis's arms were covered with a variety of tattoos. Most were roughly drawn and in black ink.

Prison tattoos.

A couple of others, though, were colorful and elaborate, done by professionals with a keen eye and a steady hand.

One in particular showed five playing cards, a poker hand.

Aces and eights.

A dead man's hand.

"You play poker, gringo?"

"Better than you."

He laughed again. This man in front of him was plain loco.

The door opened again. It was one of Luis's flunkies and Tony.

Tony smiled broadly when he saw Luis's men flanking Dave and holding his arms.

He tried to diffuse the situation.

"Dave, Dave, Dave... I warned you not to talk about Luis's sister. I told you he's very sensitive about that. Yes, she's a fine mamacita. But have some respect, will you?"

Luis laughed again.

"You need glasses, Tony. Carmen is as ugly as a mangy coyote. But if you want I can fix her up with you."

"Thanks, Luis, but I have my heart set on someone else. Did I miss anything good?"

"The gringo and I were trying to decide whether we want to play darts or poker."

"Darts? You weren't threatening my new partner with that old darts gag of yours, were you?"

"You should have seen the fear in his eyes."

Tony looked at Dave and said, "I thought you were fearless, Dave. Were you afraid?"

"Only enough to piss my pants."

Luis roared and went to Dave, then told his thugs, "Let him go."

He put his arm around Dave and said, "You're okay for a gringo. You're not too bright. But that's okay. I like my gringos dumb so I can push them around easier."

"That's me. Just a big, dumb, easy to push around gringo."

Tony asked, "So, what about the red pickup truck. You guys seen it?"

"No. If one of my men saw something like that he'd have told me about it and asked if I wanted it. It's never been on our turf or I'd know about it.

"But we'll keep an eye out for it. That is..."

He turned to Dave and said, "That is if there's a finders fee."

Dave's confidence was coming back.

"A finder's fee? What are you, the Frito Bandito?"

Luis roared again and said, "You know what, Tony? I'm starting to like this guy. He's way funnier than you. Not bad for a lily-white cornbread-fed cabron."

Tony smiled at Dave and said, "You've won him over, partner. When Luis calls you cabron, you're practically part of his family."

"Okay. But what does it mean?"

"You're better off not knowing."

"I'll tell you what, gringos. We'll keep an eye out for your pickup truck. If we find it, we'll tell you where it is. For one case of Cuervo for my man who finds it. And two cases for me."

Tony said, "Write that down, Dave. A case of fifths for his man, two cases of fifths for Luis."

"Screw fifths, Tony. Liters. Two cases of liters." A fifth won't even whet my thirst."

"Okay, Luis. You win. Just please, tell your men not to shoot the people in the pickup."

"Why in hell not?"

"Because they've got kids in the pickup with them. And too many kids have died already."

Luis suddenly grew solemn.

He crossed himself, as though remembering his own lost loved ones.

"You have my word, gringo. Now get the hell out of here before I pull out my darts and start warming up."

"Okay, okay. I'll be back on Tuesday."

"Adios, my friends."

They were the kindest words Dave had heard since his arrival.

## Chapter 18

"Mom, why do you think he hasn't called us yet?"

Lindsey was in tears. She hadn't slept well in several nights, and had been depressed and moody.

Sarah knew something was bothering her daughter, but she wasn't opening up about it.

She was ready to write it off as merely a teenaged girl being a teenaged girl.

Then she walked by Lindsey's bunk to see her staring intently at the only photograph they had of Dave. It was the Texas driver's license he left behind because it finally dawned on him he no longer needed it.

Then Lindsey's moodiness suddenly made sense.

Sarah entered the cubicle Lindsey had come to hate and normally only used to sleep in.

Or when she wanted to be alone for a bit.

She sat on her daughter's bed and took her hand.

Lindsey sat upright and fell into her mom's shoulder, the tears coming unashamedly.

"He said he was going to call. But he's been gone for over two weeks now. He hasn't called once. Do you think they killed him, Mom? Do you think he's dead? Do you think we'll ever see him or Beth again?"

"Shhhh... look at me."

Sarah took her by the shoulders and held her at arm's length.

"No. Don't look down, honey. Lift up your chin and look at me. I want to make sure you understand every word I'm saying."

They locked eyes.

"Honey, you know your father. If he said he's going to do something, he'll do it. But you also know that ham radios are few and far between. The only people who have them are preppers who had the foresight to protect them. And those types of people tend to keep a low profile. He might go for days or even weeks without coming across one. And even when he does, there's no guarantee they'll let him use their radio.

"I wouldn't, if I were them. Because in order for him to use their radio they'd have to let him into their compound, or bunker, or wherever their radio was.

"Your father is a wonderful man, Lindsey. I love him with all my heart. You know that. But he can be a scary looking dude when he hasn't shaved or had a haircut in awhile. He smells like a bear when he hasn't showered in more than a day. He farts and has stinky feet.

"In short, your father can look and smell like Bigfoot. Would *you* let him into your compound to use the radio if you were a prepper and didn't know him?"

Sarah's words had the desired effect.

Lindsey smiled.

Her face was still soaked in tears, but she felt a bit better.

"No. Maybe not."

"And you also know your father well enough to know he can develop tunnel vision when he's working on something important.

"Right now his sights are focused like a laser on finding Beth. That's his number one priority, and the thing that will guide everything he does. You and I, as much as he loves us, will take a back seat until he has some spare time and gets around to us.

"That may sound harsh and a bit cold, but that's the way it has to be. Beth needs him more than we do now, because he knows we're safe.

"At some point he'll have some free time, and then he'll look for a ham radio. And he'll use his charm to try to convince them to let him use it.

"Then he'll contact us. Until then, though, we have to remain strong. For each other."

"That's easy for you to say, Mom. You're the strongest person I know. Even stronger than Dad.

You've always been the rock of the family. Even Dad's told me that."

"Has he really?"

"Yes. But he said if I ever told you he'd deny it."

"Honey, you wouldn't think I was such a rock if you knew I cried myself to sleep every night. I worry about Beth. I worry about your father. I worry about us and how we'll survive if we never see either of them again."

"You too? You've considered that possibility too?"

"Of course I have. I'd have to have my head buried deeply in the sand to not think about it."

"I'm going to ask you something very silly, Mom. Don't be afraid to tell me I'm an idiot."

"I would never tell you that, honey. Even if you were. Which you're not, by the way. What did you want to ask?"

"Like you said, the nights are particularly hard. Some nights I lay here for hours trying to fall asleep, but I just can't get them out of my mind. I've been tempted several times to just come over to your cubicle and crawl into bed with you. But I didn't know how you'd feel about it."

"Oh, honey, I wish I'd known. Of course you can come over and join me. You always did that, whenever you had a bad dream or you weren't feeling well. Do you remember that time when you crawled into bed with your father and I and he asked if you were okay…"

Lindsey finished her sentence for her.

"… and I threw up all over him and he caught his breath and said, 'Well, I guess not.'"

The two of them shared a much-needed laugh.

"I know I used to all the time, Mom. But not since I was seven. I'm sixteen now, and almost grown up. I don't want you to get the idea I'm still a baby or something."

"Oh, honey… you'll always be my baby, no matter how old you get."

She held her daughter close.

"From now on, any time you can't sleep for any reason, you come and crawl into bed with me. If that doesn't comfort you enough to help you sleep, we'll just talk long into the night."

"Until we bore each other to sleep?"

"Exactly."

"Oh, and Lindsey?"

"Yes, ma'am?"

"If you throw up on me like you did your father, I'll kick your butt. I don't play."

## Chapter 19

It was mere coincidence that at the exact moment Lindsey and Sarah were discussing ham radios, Tony told Dave he had one.

Or maybe it was a higher power intervening in a difficult situation.

And it didn't really matter. For Dave couldn't have been happier if God himself appeared from the heavens and placed a brand spanking new ham radio unit at Dave's feet.

"You're kidding!"

"Why would I kid about something like that?"

"Good point. But where did you get a ham radio?"

"Duh. From the same guy I got the Polaris from. He's a big time prepper. He traded me the radio for two eight balls."

"Two eight balls? As in pool balls?"

"No, dummy. Two eight balls of meth. An eight ball is an eighth of an ounce. Three and a half grams."

"It's probably a good thing I didn't know that."

"You're such an innocent, Dave. Being seen with you is probably bad for my reputation."

"Funny. I thought the opposite was true."

"Hardly."

"So, why did you need a ham radio?"

"I thought I might be able to communicate with some... friends... I know in Georgia. But they apparently don't have a radio. I spoke to one guy that was about a hundred miles from them, but that was the closest hit I got. And he said he wouldn't get a message to them for any amount of money in the world."

"Wanna sell it?"

Tony looked at him as though he'd suddenly grown another head.

And Dave realized what a stupid question he'd just asked.

He wished he could take back his words, but it was too late. He now had to listen to Tony give him a royal rash.

"What in hell are you going to do with a ham radio, Dave? You live in an abandoned truck, for cryin' out loud. Everything you have in the world is in a damn backpack.

"Are you gonna tell your underwear and extra socks to move over and make room, so you can stuff a ham radio into your backpack as well?

"And who are you gonna talk to anyway? You said the only person you have left is your daughter, and you don't even know where in hell she is. And I doubt she's carrying her own ham radio around with her in her back pocket."

Tony suddenly brought his diatribe to a screeching halt.

He'd meant to be funny. He'd meant to give his new friend a hard time for asking a stupid question.

But he'd gone way too far. His words weren't funny, they were hurtful.

And they were unnecessary. All they did was to remind Dave what a dire predicament he was in. That his young daughter was out there, somewhere, in the custody of brutal slave-owners, being made to do God-only knew what to survive each miserable day.

"I'm sorry, Dave."

The apology was simple yet sincere.

Dave accepted it without comment, merely nodding his head.

The truth was, not a waking hour went by that he wondered what little Beth was doing at that very moment.

And he fought constantly with a very dark and very evil part of his mind, which was constantly telling him he was a fool. That Beth was dead, and he'd never find her tiny body. Never be able to cry over her. Never know what happened to her and why.

Tony tried to make amends.

"Look… Dave. Why don't you come back with me to my place? I have plenty of room. You can stay with me while we finish our sweep of Albuquerque. And yes, you can use my ham radio. You cannot buy it, no. I still have plans to use it again at a later date. To try again to find someone in Georgia close enough to my friends to get a message to them.

"And you couldn't use it anyway without an antenna and a generator. And you couldn't fit an antenna and generator in your backpack no matter how much your socks and underwear gave way."

This time his humor was kinder and gentler.

And this time it worked.

Dave smiled and said, "I guess it was a stupid question, wasn't it?"

"Damn straight, partner."

## Chapter 20

On the long journey from Albuquerque to Tony's place in the suburbs, Dave came clean to his friend about his family's situation.

There were some things he kept to himself, though.

Like the operable Ford Explorer he had parked not far away.

"I'll tell you what," Tony offered. "When we get to my place I'll put you up in the guest room. And I'll show you where the ham radio is. While I'm cooking us up some supper you can move the radio to your own room and call your family."

Tony almost broke down and confessed about his own family, and how he wondered every day whether they were alive or dead.

But once again he chose to keep it to himself.

He did admit to one thing, though.

"I have to say, Dave, I'm impressed."

"About what?"

"I was already impressed that you struck out from Kansas and came all the way to Albuquerque to find your daughter. That took a lot of dedication and a shitload of guts.

"But now you tell me that Kansas wasn't where you started out. That you had already walked all the way from Texas to get there. I gotta  say, you're either the craziest son of a bitch who ever walked the earth, or the most dedicated father ever."

"I don't know about that, Tony. I'd crawl through the fires of hell to save one of my children. I think any father would."

Tony fell silent and looked away.

The sun was getting low in the sky now. Darkness was almost upon them.

Tony used that to his advantage, to help hide the tears in his eyes. And he used the breeze, rushing into his face as he steered the Polaris down the street at fifteen miles an hour, to help dry them.

Finally, thankfully, the conversation came to an end when Tony turned into the driveway of a modest two-story home half a mile outside the Albuquerque city limits.

Dave wasn't sure what he was expecting, exactly. Maybe a crack house, with dope fiends hanging around, anxiously awaiting their master of moods and purveyor of poisons.

That's how he'd always pictured the way drug dealers must live.

He knew very little about the game. Basically what he'd seen on *Cops* and other shows like it.

He knew there was a lot of money in the drug game. And that dealers usually got rich.

But he also knew there was a lot of risk involved as well. That regardless of how careful they were, how untouchable they claimed to be, they were always caught eventually.

And then they went to prison and lost everything.

Dave believed the smart ones read the writing on the wall. That they served their time and got out of the business and tried another means of making a living.

But Dave really was a babe in the woods when it came to the drug culture. An "innocent," as Tony had laughingly called him.

Dave didn't understand the harsh realities of the game. That most drug dealers went that route because it was easy. And because their other options were extremely limited.

Dave didn't know that most of them had no education, and no prospects to get one. Most didn't even have fathers. And unless they wanted to flip hamburgers the rest of their lives, their only other options were to deal drugs or steal.

He also didn't know that even the option of flipping burgers went away once a drug dealer was released from prison.

Not even fast food joints would hire a convicted felon.

That left essentially two options for a newly released convict, even if he had seen the writing on the wall... stealing or returning to the game.

For most dealers, therefore, it was a sadistic dance. In and out of the joint, on and off the streets. And when they were on the streets they were dealing.

Because that was all they knew and they had no prospects for doing anything else.

As they approached the house the sniper on the roof stood up and revealed himself. He waved at Tony, who waved back. A man who'd been hidden in the shrubbery walked out to greet his boss as well.

"This is Dave. He'll be staying with me for a few days."

Dave could tell from the shocked look on the man's face that Tony didn't bring home a lot of houseguests.

The man nodded but didn't introduce himself. Tony didn't introduce him either.

For Dave he'd just remain a nameless man who hid in the bushes to protect his friend and his property.

It didn't exactly give Dave a warm fuzzy. But at least Tony knew the security risks of being in possession of large quantities of drugs and was taking measures to protect himself.

As they walked into the house, Dave observed, "So... I'm guessing you don't bring strangers home very often to stay with you."

"No. Occasionally a girl I want to spend time with. In fact, you're the first guy I've ever brought home."

Dave suddenly laughed.

"What? What's so funny?"

"Maybe that's why the guy in the bushes looked so shocked. Maybe he thinks you're switching sides."

Tony smiled.

"You think he thinks I'm gay? He knows me better than that. They all do."

"Good," Dave said. "Because I'm going on record here and now by saying you're not my type. I don't care how good you might cook."

## Chapter 21

"Jonas or Jacob, this is Sarah's husband Dave. Come in if you read me."

Jacob was sitting in front of the base station when the call came in. He didn't recognize Dave's voice, but then again he hadn't spent a lot of time with him before he left.

Still, it had to be him. It could have been a coincidence that someone was calling Jonas or Jacob. There were probably a lot of Jonases and Jacobs in the world who were using ham radios.

But it was too much of a stretch to think those Jonases and Jacobs also knew a Sarah who happened to be married to a Dave.

He figured it was safe to answer.

"This is Jacob. Go ahead, Dave, but just a reminder. Don't give any details as to either of our locations."

"You got it, Jacob. How are things going there?"

"By how are things going you mean how are Sarah and Lindsey?"

"Yeah, well, that would have been my next question."

"Things are good. *They* are good. I'm gonna put the microphone down so I can go get them."

"Thank you, sir."

"No problem. Be back in a flash."

Dave looked around the guest room, and his eyes caught an eight by ten framed photograph on the bedside table.

A professional photo, taken at a sitting in one of the local portrait studios.

A portrait of happier times.

They were seated on the floor, the two of them. A slightly younger Tony and the knockout blonde at his side.

Between them two little boys wore their Sunday-best suits. They had their mother's smile, their father's facial features.

They looked incredibly happy, the four of them.

So, this wasn't just some abandoned house Tony had claimed as his own.

Dave wondered about the family. What became of them. Whether they were alive or dead.

For a brief second, he thought he might ask Tony about them.

But no. He wouldn't. Tony had already had plenty of opportunities to mention he had a family. He hadn't done so. And that probably meant he didn't have a family. Not anymore.

That made Dave sad. And he realized how lucky he was in that his family was all still alive.

As far as he knew.

His attention was called back to the radio when a familiar voice came sputtering through the speakers.

It was a voice as smooth and soothing as butter. A voice he'd said goodnight to thousands of times. A voice which brought a smile to his face.

"Dave, are you there?"

"Hi, honey. How are you?"

"Better, now. I've been missing you. Lindsey has too. We've been wrecks lately, hoping each new day would bring a renewed chance you'd call us. Do you have good news?"

"No, I haven't found her yet. I've got some good leads I'm running down. And I know I'm getting close. But you'll have to give me a little more time, I'm afraid."

"I understand. And I don't guess you can tell me where you are?"

"Not specifically, no. Not far from your Aunt Edna's. Want me to stop by and say hello?"

"You wouldn't get any response, Dave. Not since she died five years ago."

"Well, even when she was alive she ignored me most of the time. She didn't much like me, and I never figured out why."

"Don't feel bad, honey. She never really liked anybody. And thanks for the hint, by the way."

"No problem. Don't worry about the Beth thing, honey. I'll find her if I have to spend the rest of my days looking. And I'll bring her home to you. And she'll be walking and talking and laughing just as she's always done."

"Dave, please don't make promises you may not be able to keep."

"Oh, but I have every intention of keeping that promise. She's still alive. I know it. And I'll bring her back, you see."

## Chapter 22

Dave was a bit melancholy when he left the guest room and met Tony in the kitchen.

The kitchen was equipped with a wood burning stove, which Dave knew from personal experience was one of the hardest contraptions ever invented to master.

"Was that with the house before the blackout?"

"Yes. My wife..."

It was a slip of the tongue that gave so much away, yet left so much more unanswered.

But he was committed.

"My wife was a chef. She cooked on wood sometimes because she said the flavor couldn't be matched on some things. Like these steaks. I have a natural gas stove too, but it's pretty much worthless these days."

Dave waited for more, but there was no more coming.

So he turned his attention to the steaks.

"Well those smell pretty damn good, so she must have known what she was talking about. If you tell me they're human, though, I'm walking out of the joint."

"Nope. That's something I'll never do is stoop so low I'll eat human flesh. I know there are some out there who do. But I'm not one of them."

"So where'd you get the steaks?"

"From a rancher I know who happens to have a cocaine habit. He craves blow. I crave beef. It's a pretty good arrangement."

"And the house?"

"I bought the house six years ago. Are you surprised?"

"A little bit, yes. Was that before..."

"Before I started selling dope? Yes. This house, as a matter of fact, was one of the reasons I started selling. I got laid off about the same time a good friend of mine got busted for manufacturing. I knew where he stashed two kilos of meth. He was going away for twenty years, and it seemed too good an opportunity to pass up.

"It was either that or going homeless. The bank, you see, wants to get its money and has very little tolerance for excuses."

"And your friend? He didn't mind?"

"Like I said, he was going away for twenty. And as it turned out, he went away for life instead."

"Oh?"

"He was stabbed to death in prison."

"Oh."

"The funny thing is, he wasn't confrontational. Not at all. I knew him for years and he was a peacemaker. They had a gang war going on when he got there. One night they piled bunks against the door of the pod to keep the correctional officers out for a few minutes. Then all the shanks came out and started flying.

"As I understand it, he tried to stop it. He cornered his own leader. The pod leader, a big dude named Bubba. He tried to convince him it wasn't worth it.

"Bubba stabbed him. His own guy. For trying to keep the peace. The other guys pounced on him too. Said he was a traitor. Left the blacks just watching, amazed that the whites would turn on their own like they did.

"Anyway, the guards finally got the door open and came in with an assault team. There were a couple of other guys on both sides who were bloody. But only my friend died."

It was obviously a fresh wound.

And Dave didn't know what else to say.

So he changed the subject.

"What was your wife's name?"

Silence, then: "That's a subject I don't talk about."

"Fair enough. I won't bring it up again. But if you ever do want to talk about it, I'm a good listener."

"How do you want your steak?"

It turned out Dave wasn't the only one adept at changing the subject.

"Medium well. Anything I can do to help?"

"Yes. As a matter of fact, how about peeling those four potatoes over there? Then slice them up and put them in the blue pan. There's some vegetable oil in the first cupboard."

"French fries? Wow. I haven't had fries in well over a year. Should I ask where you got the potatoes? No, wait, let me guess. You have a farmer friend with a wicked affection for crack?"

"Not even close. I grow them myself."

"You're kidding."

"Nope. I'm not. Go look out the back door. See for yourself."

Curious, Dave walked over to a sliding glass patio door and pulled back the draperies.

Sure enough, the back yard was a lush green, with a variety of plants.

And not only that, it was huge.

As though Tony read his mind, he elaborated.

"The house behind me and on either side of me were abandoned. No, I didn't chase anybody out. It just worked out that way.

"But I didn't waste any time in taking advantage of the situation. I had a couple of guys tear down all the fences so I could turn all four yards into my personal garden. It's my hobby. It's what I do when I'm not meeting with my suppliers or making my deliveries."

"But... don't you need a special type of soil to grow potatoes?"

"Well, you need a better soil than we have here, for damn sure. I paid those same two guys to take my Polaris when I wasn't using it. It took them almost four weeks off and on. But they were able to go to a soil company half a mile away and haul back about four tons of rich topsoil a little at a time.

"Then we mixed it with the soil I had, and made something that was pretty respectable for growing most vegetables.

"For what I call the soft beds, where I grow my potatoes, peanuts, radishes and carrots, we mixed in forty eight bags of potting soil as well. It softened the earth and keeps it from clumping and choking everything out. And it added a lot of nutrients that make everything grow bigger."

## Chapter 23

"But why?"

"Why what?"

"You can have people bring you food. Why do you go through all the trouble of growing your own?"

"I was a health food nut even before the blackout. That's why I don't use any of the dope I sell. I figured even after the blackout I gotta eat. I can eat the canned goods from the trucks and hope they're not tainted. Or I can grow my own food and know it's safe.

"Besides, it gives me something to do. I can't watch TV anymore.

"Well, I could. I mean, my prepper friend brought me a TV and DVD player and a box full of DVDs to watch. But I never was much of a movie guy. I liked sports and nature shows. And those things no longer exist.

"Watching my plants grow is my nature show now. Wrestling the crops out of the ground is my sport."

After dinner they retired to the den.

"Sit down, Dave. We're going into the lion's den in the morning. The worst of the worst. We need to discuss strategy.

"Would you like a drink?"

"Sure. What do you have?"

"A little bit of everything. I'm a dope dealer, remember? I can get things other people can't."

"Whiskey is fine."

"Neat?"

"Ice, if you have it."

"Oh, I definitely have it."

"On second thought, How about a glass of ice and a bottle of water? I haven't had ice water in a year, and I can't imagine anything possibly tasting better than that."

"You got it."

Tony dropped ice cubes into a tall glass. Just the sound of the cubes against the side of the glass made Dave's mouth water.

It occurred to him that one didn't truly appreciate the simple things in life until they were taken away from them.

Tony poured himself a double shot of whiskey.

"I thought you all about being healthy," Dave remarked.

"This is my one and only guilty pleasure. And I never drink to excess. One double each evening to relax me and knock off the road dust. That's all."

"Yet you surround yourself with people who cannot control their urges or their addictions. Are you ever tempted to just break down and say the hell with it and get totally wasted?"

"No. That would be an end to my hopes and dreams."

"You're set. You live like a king. At least, compared to nearly everybody else out there. What could you possibly have hopes and dreams about?"

"Another thing I'd rather not talk about. Let's just say that someday soon I plan to take a journey. A very long journey, to try to recover some things from my past.

"Some things that were very dear to me."

"Wow. Could you possibly be any more mysterious?"

Tony laughed.

"Probably not. But you have to understand, Dave, that I'm a very private man. It doesn't appear that way, I know..."

"Ya think? Everybody on this side of town either knows you or knows of you. People run for you when they hear your vehicle approaching. You're the closest thing I've seen to a celebrity since the lights went out."

Tony sighed.

"That's all true, yes. But that's not the way I intended it. They run for me because I can give them something to ease their pain. At least for awhile. I can help them escape reality. It's not because they like me. Many of them hate me. But I have something many of them need."

"You said we needed to plan, because we were going into a very bad place. Where, exactly, are we going?"

"Into the pits of hell, I believe is the phrase I used. The only part of Albuquerque I'm afraid to go into."

"Why? I thought all the factions gave you safe passage."

"They do. Even this one does. But they're real iffy. And they're the only ones in the whole city who don't seem to be afraid of killing me and starting a turf war. That's because they're crazy sons of bitches. And because they like to kill."

"Who is 'they,' exactly?"

"They're called Dalton's Raiders. They came from Alabama. Good old boys. Only they're not so good. They patterned themselves after some of the renegade Confederate armies of the civil war. The ones which stormed into the southern cities and raped and pillaged and killed, and then burned the cities to the ground on their way out.

"Before the lights went out they were merely a biker gang. They were run by a man named Dalton. Nobody knows his first name, and nobody has the guts to ask. They were based out of Birmingham before the blackout, and even the local cops were afraid of them. Every time one of them got arrested, a cop's family member disappeared within a couple of months. Just disappeared without a trace, never to be seen again. After it happened for the fourth time the cops finally put two and two together and realized the two things were connected. The Raiders never took credit for the disappearances, or bragged about it even to other gangs. But everybody knew what was going on.

"Finally, the cops just stopped arresting them. The word got around that as long as they didn't kill or maim somebody, the cops would let everything else slide.

"The Raiders were king of the mountain after that point. They literally owned Birmingham.

"Then the blackout happened and screwed everything up. The cops who lost family members formed their own gang, with other cops who hated the Raiders. They started shooting them from rooftops with sniper rifles.

"Dalton lost a third of his boys before he got smart and got the hell out of Dodge. Or Birmingham, I guess."

"So what did they do?"

"They swept their way west on horseback. Horses they stole from a rancher, after they shot his seven member family dead. And they did just like the rogue armies did in the confederate days. They left death and destruction in their wake."

"Finally, six months ago, they landed here."

## Chapter 24

"Okay, so they're bad dudes. But what makes them worse than the other factions?"

"Dalton is insane. I mean certifiably so. As in, the dangerous kind of insane. Men like that usually don't gain power of a group the size of his and keep it very long. Usually other members of the group will take advantage of their leader's craziness, find a weak spot, and exploit it. They'll overthrow him and usually kill him in the process.

"In this case, most of his lieutenants are as insane as he is. I don't know how it turned out that way, but most of his muscle should have been locked up long ago. In the kind of cells with padding on the walls.

"They're like sharks in a frenzy. They feed off each other. One will come up with a crazy idea. Like, for example, they'll go through the neighborhoods and burn down every third house. Even if there are people inside.

"Just for the fun of it.

"And then another one will up the ante. He'll say that in addition to burning every third house, they'll shoot every third person who comes running out of a burning house.

"Another one will say, 'Okay, that's all well and good. But our guys are horny. So in addition to shooting every third person, we'll capture every fourth person and rape them. Man, woman or child, it doesn't matter."

Dave was skeptical.

"Okay, so they're all crazy enough to come up with such plans. But do you think they'd actually do it?"

"That's just it, Dave. I know for a fact they would. Because I've seen them do all kinds of crazy shit. A month ago they called every one of their men together for a loyalty test. They all drew numbers and the five with the lowest numbers got sent out of their territory late that night.

"They had simple instructions: They were each to bring back the head of a rival faction member. They didn't care how they obtained the heads, as long as they were back before sunrise with their trophies."

"And if they didn't make it?"

"They were told that if they didn't make it back they weren't to come back. That they were no longer a member of the Raiders and that they'd be shot on sight."

"Ouch. That's kinda harsh."

"And they meant it, too. One of them didn't make it back until after sunrise. The shot him in the gut and let him bleed to death in front of them.

"He begged them to shoot him in the head, to put him out of his misery. Dalton laughed at him and said he didn't want to mess up his 'pretty little head.' Dalton wanted to preserve it. And sure enough, his head got put on a stake, right next to the head he'd brought back with him.

"I heard that Dalton went around singing a little song and dancing, because he got a 'twofer' out of the deal. Two heads instead of one.

"I'm serious, Dave. This is the only area in Albuquerque I hate to go into. Because even though I supply many of their men with drugs, I figure it's only a matter of time before they kill me."

"So why don't we just go in there last? Then if we find the pickup before then we won't have to go in at all."

Dave smiled and crossed his arms in front of him, sure that he'd come up with the perfect solution.

And proud of himself for coming up with it before Tony did.

But it turned out Dave wasn't as smart as he believed himself to be.

"You don't get it, Dave. I have to go in there. I have no choice. I have my regular deliveries to make. And there's another reason we need to go."

"What's that?"

"This is the last territory in Albuquerque that's adjacent to Interstate 40. We've covered all the rest and nobody has seen your horse drawn pickup."

"And that's important why, again?"

"Because you said they came into the city on I-40, headed west. If they ever left the highway and entered Albuquerque, they had to have entered in Dalton's Raiders' territory. It's the only place left for them to have exited the highway. We've covered all the other bases."

Dave suddenly got a knot in the pit of his stomach. And he shuddered when he thought of his Beth being subjected to the wanton cruelty of the men Tony just described.

## Chapter 25

Dave was frightened. Not for himself, for he was a hardened combat veteran who feared no man.

No, he was frightened for Beth.

He had to have the answer to a single question. And he dreaded what it might be.

"Have they been known to harm children?"

"Not to my knowledge, no. That may be the only line they haven't yet crossed. But..."

"But what?"

"But they won't hesitate for a second to shoot the old couple driving the wagon. Either to take the wagon from them, or just out of meanness or boredom."

"But... if they did that... if they shot the old couple, what would happen to Beth?"

"I don't know, Dave. I suppose they'd likely make a slave out of her. Make her do their cooking and cleaning for them."

Tony went no further than that. But silently he was thinking the same thoughts Dave was.

That such brutal and sadistic men might not settle for Beth doing their chores.

That they could rob her of her innocence and her dignity.

No, Dave wasn't afraid for himself, even if going up against a thousand such men.

But he was afraid for his daughter.

And he was ready for war, or anything short of it, to get her safely back where she belonged.

"Okay. So what's our plan?"

"I was thinking about it on the way back from town. I think it's a good one, but you're not gonna like it."

"There's absolutely nothing about this whole situation I like. Tell me about it."

"I'm going in without you."

"You're what?"

"Hear me out, Dave. You heard what the other factions said about me bringing you onto their turf. They all bitched about it because they don't like strangers. They don't trust them.

"We were able to talk our way in despite that distrust because the other factions are run by more or less reasonable people."

"Luis didn't seem so reasonable when he said he was going to cut off my head and throw darts at it."

"As big and bad and scary as Luis was, Dave, he's a pussycat compared to these guys. If we go in there together there's a good chance their gatekeepers will just blow us away before we can get a word out to explain.

"And if we do get past the sentries, Dalton will probably order us executed. Just for having the nerve to deviate from his usual comfort zone.

"And since your daughter's only chance of being rescued lies in you, you won't be doing her any favors by getting yourself killed. You'll be condemning her to a hard and miserable life. A life in which she'll wonder each and every day why you never came after her. Because she likely won't know that you tried and died."

"Okay. You have my undivided attention. What's the whole plan?"

"Like I said, I worry every time I go in there. But I've been lucky and managed to get back out every time so far.

"I have a much better chance of coming out if I go in alone. The I-40 is no-man's land. It doesn't belong to any one faction. That's because they decided early on to leave the highway open to let travelers pass through instead of taking shortcuts through their territories. That's why they have their names painted on cars at all the highway exits. To warn people not to leave the highway."

"Okay. With you so far..."

"I'll drop you off on the highway, before we get to the Dalton's Raiders' exit. You can pretend you're a highway nomad, and just hang around one of the abandoned trucks like you're looking for socks or something.

"I'll go in and do my normal drops. And while I'm there I'll tell them I heard about the red pickup drawn by two horses and ask if they've seen it. They're much more likely to tell me where it is than they'd tell you. You're an outsider. At least they know me."

"Okay. Then what?"

"They'll demand to know why I'm looking for it. And I'll tell them the same story as before. That I'm going to start running hooch. But that my Polaris isn't big enough. So I'll tell them I'll start coming twice a week. One day to deliver my dope on the Polaris. And that I'll take orders for the hooch on that day. I'll come back on another day, late in the same week, in the red wagon. And the red pickup will be loaded down with liquor."

"Okay, let me play devil's advocate here. Once you find out where the pickup is, won't it look suspicious if you just leave without it?"

"Probably. So what I'll do is go find it. I'll tell the old couple I don't want to buy it. I want to lease it. I'll tell them I don't know beans about how to drive a horse drawn pickup truck, or how to take care of horses.

"I'll tell them I'll pay them handsomely to drive the wagon outside of Dalton's territory to a warehouse where I have all the liquor stashed. I'll tell them they can help me load it, and then they can go with me to deliver it all one day a week.

"Whatever they want, I'll promise to pay them. If they want gold, I'll agree to their terms. But I'll negotiate just a little to make it look good. If they want to be paid in dope or booze, I'll make that deal too."

"Okay. Then what?"

"If we come to terms, I'll try to get them to follow me out of their territory. To drive the pickup behind me. Once we're safely away, we'll turn east on I-40. I'll tell them my warehouse is just a few miles away."

Dave finished the thought for him.

"And once you're on I-40, you'll come right past me."

"Exactly. You'll see us coming half a mile away, but will stay under cover behind a truck or something until we pass by. Then you can walk up behind them. I'll ride slightly behind them on the other side. We'll draw our weapons at the same time and get the drop on them.

"There won't be a damn thing they can do, besides stop and surrender your daughter."

## Chapter 26

Dave thought hard for several minutes trying to poke holes in the plan but couldn't. It was a good plan indeed.

And it should work.

It had to work.

He could think of only one thing that might go wrong.

"What if they want to think about it first? After all, you'll be a stranger just coming in out of nowhere, asking them to go to some strange place. They may not trust you."

"I thought of that. If they do want to think about it, or want to wet their beak up front, I can work around that too."

"Wet their what?"

"It's an old Sicilian term. It means a taste. A taste of the goods. A kickback. They may not think I really have a warehouse full of liquor. They may say, bring us a case of Old Crow and a case of Dom so we'll know you're not just blowing smoke."

"And if they do that?"

"Then I'll play their game. I'll get a case of each from one of my contacts, and I'll take it to them as a gift. Hopefully it'll whet their appetites and convince them I'm on the up and up. And if I can get them to come with me, the end result is the same. You'll be waiting out here and we can get the drop on them. Take your daughter back without a shot being fired."

"Okay. It's a plan."

"Food's done. Let's eat and get a good night's sleep. Tomorrow's gonna be a big day, and if all goes well we'll be setting a third plate for your daughter tomorrow night."

"Are you a praying man, Tony?"

"No. I stopped believing in God a long time ago."

"Can I ask why?"

"I'll give you the basics, as long as you don't ask for details."

"Okay."

"Everything and everybody I ever loved, I lost. Some due to death, some to illness, some to my own stupidity. I've spent my whole life trying to be a good person. I didn't always play by the rules. But they were man's rules. Not the rules of your God. I never hurt anyone. Not intentionally. I generally tried to help people, as I'm helping you now.

"I would think that someone who tried to be good, who tried not to hurt anyone, would be rewarded in some way. Yet every time I fell in love I got heartbroken. Every time I tried to do something good I got punished. Every time I trusted a friend, I was betrayed. Everyone I ever loved, who ever loved me, is gone.

"Now, I don't know what one has to do to be in good graces with your God. But I'm tired of waiting for something divine to happen in my life and getting stomped on. If this is the way your God treats someone who tries his best to be good, I'm not so sure I want anything to do with Him."

This was not the time to get into a long theological debate. There were more pressing matters to contend with.

But that didn't mean Dave would give up on his friend.

"Can we talk about this another time, Tony? Maybe give me a chance to show you a side you maybe haven't considered?"

"I'll always talk. What else do we have to do?"

"Good. I may be able to help you see the light."

"Right now, Dave, the only light I see is an oncoming train. One that's threatening to mow me down."

"You're my partner now, Tony. I'll kick that train's ass before it has a chance."

Tony smiled.

"Can I ask you something, Dave?"

"Sure. Ask away."

"You say you do believe in God…"

"Yes."

"But you've killed."

"Every time I've killed it was in self defense. Or to rescue my family, who they were holding hostage."

"But the Bible says 'Thou shalt not kill.' It doesn't list exceptions. At least I don't remember any when my folks forced me to go to church. How do you reconcile that?"

"I've asked God for forgiveness and asked for his mercy."

"So you think he'll grant you a waiver based on circumstances?"

"That's my hope, yes."

"What about when you have no such excuse?"

"What do you mean?"

"When we get the drop on the couple who kidnapped your daughter and turned her into a slave, what do you plan to do with them?"

"I've thought about that a lot, actually. I think I'm going to take them out into the desert, far from civilization. I'm going to tie them to stakes and let them die of thirst."

"On desert sands? Sounds sort of Biblical to me."

"Exactly."

Dave hesitated. His words of bravado sounded harsh, even to him.

"And you think your God would forgive you for that?"

He paused, then admitted, "Probably not."

"There's one more thing we haven't discussed."

"What's that?"

"Before we leave here in the morning I'm going to draw you a map."

"Of what and why?"

"Just in case. You were a Marine, didn't you say?"

"Yes."

"So was my dad. He loved being a Marine. He told me all kinds of stories about his Marine days when I was a kid. He taught me how to use a rifle, and some self-defense techniques. He loved the Corps."

"So did I. I hope they can recover. It would be a shame to lose them after all this time."

"My dad taught me something else about the Corps."

"What was that?"

"He said Marines always had a Plan B. And then a Plan C. Contingency plans for their contingency plans, he called them."

Dave smiled.

"Well, that's true enough."

"The map is in case they kill me. So you'll know where to find Dalton and his leaders so you can deal with them another way."

## Chapter 27

On a sprawling ranch outside of Adelanto, California a 1982 Ford Ranger pickup sat gathering dust in the late afternoon sun.

A lizard sat dead center on the roof of the vehicle, soaking up the last rays of the sun, and hoping a passing fly might come within reach of his tongue.

One of the pickup's tires was flat now, but it didn't matter much anymore. The wheels hadn't rolled in three months, and likely never would again.

The pickup had served its purpose. It had gotten Old Sal and Nellie to the high desert of southern California. In another era this land, sandwiched between Edwards Air Force Base, George Air Force Base and Lancaster, played a key role in the race to space and the moon.

Test pilots flew all manner of experimental aircraft through these skies.

This place, the city of Adelanto, was where puzzled residents went outside their homes and looked skyward after hearing the very first sonic boom.

The boom was created when Chuck Yeager first broke the sound barrier in the skies above them. But they didn't know that. All they knew was they heard what sounded like an explosion. Their walls and dishes shook. Their dogs barked. Their babies cried.

They'd heard things like that in the past, when a test pilot's luck ran out and he crashed into the ground.

The Air Force didn't like that word: "crashed."

They preferred the term "impacted with ground." It was more aesthetically pleasing.

But it meant the same thing.

The people in Adelanto, and in nearby Victorville, came out of their homes and looked around for the smoke of a crashed jet on that day back in 1947. They didn't see any. So they went back inside and resumed their normal activities.

Those were the glory days for the high desert. It had been in a steady decline since. Eventually George Air Force Base closed, a victim of a downsized military and congressional scrambling to close facilities and save money.

The city of Victorville suffered. The city of Adelanto almost died as United States Air Force members were transferred en masse to other places.

Sal's brother Benito, who was called Benny by everyone other than his parents, was one of the few winners.

On the day the announcement was made that George Air Force Base was closing, Benny was in his 1955 Apache pickup truck on his way home from nearby Las Vegas. On Highway 395, with his windows down and wind blowing through his hair, he heard the grim announcement on his Motorola in-dash radio.

And he laughed like a banshee.

No, he wasn't insane.

He was rich.

It didn't matter to Benny that as a civilian jet engine mechanic he would soon be out of a job.

It didn't matter that the value of his property would fall by eighty percent over the coming weeks. That many of his neighbors would declare bankruptcy. That a couple would commit suicide.

None of that would matter at all.

For he'd just hit the Super Jackpot on a ten dollar slot machine at the Lucky Lady Casino.

And he had a check for $3.2 million folded up neatly in his wallet.

In the coming months, as Victorville cried and Adelanto died, Benny thrived.

He bought several small ranches for pennies on the dollar and consolidated them into the largest ranch in San Bernardino County. He bought two thousand head of cattle from a ranch which was mired in debt, for thirty dollars a head.

Even the broken willed people of Victorville had to eat.

He was one of the few success stories in the county in the disaster that the base closure was.

And as such, his ranch was the logical place for Sal to run when the whole world fell apart. Because he knew his brother would find a way to turn the blackout to his advantage. To make big money off of it.

Benny just had that kind of luck.

They'd arrived three months before, he and Nellie and Becky.

And now they were settled in their own house on Benny's sprawling ranch. They were doing well. Helping Benny run the ranch, and reaping in the rewards.

And still trying to convince an eight year old girl that she was their grandchild.

## Chapter 28

It wasn't easy. Beth was a headstrong girl by nature, and smart beyond her years.

She knew there was something inherently wrong with a couple just buying a child and trying to convince her she was someone she knew she wasn't.

"If you wanted to brainwash somebody, you shouldn't have bought me. You should have bought yourself a baby who didn't know any better."

Her defiant tone disappointed Sal, who was raised in a family who didn't tolerate attitude. In Sal's family, insolence and defiance in children was met with a backhand across the face, followed by an evening or two sitting in the corner without supper.

But Sal had mellowed in his old age. And that was good for Beth, because it spared her the sting of his hand across her face.

Instead, he tried to reason with her, when Nellie wasn't within earshot.

"Look here, child. We didn't buy you. We adopted you. There's a big difference. The man we paid the adoption fee to said it was all legal. That they represented the state and had licenses and permits and everything else they needed to run an orphanage."

"You're a liar."

"Please don't argue with me, child. You should respect your elders, or you can't expect others to respect you when you get old like us. To get respect you must give it. Remember that, child. It's one of the most valuable of life's lessons."

She was unmoved.

"That man you talked to wasn't running an orphanage. He was keeping my mother and me and my sister hostage. He sold me and you bought me. I was not adopted. Please take me back to my mommy."

"The man at the orphanage said you've been through a lot. That you lost both your parents and your four brothers. He said you're sometimes delusional, but that it would pass with time and love and patience.

"We will be good parents to you, dear Becky. I know you can never love us as much as you did your mother and father and brothers. I know that. But someday you'll learn to love us as well. Once you see that we want only the best for you. That we provide for you, and protect you, and make sure your belly is full each night when you go to bed.

"All I ask is that you be patient with us, as we are with you."

"*Please*, stop calling me Becky. My name is Beth, and it always will be."

Part of what he was saying was the truth.

The couple did care for her, and even seemed to love her. Old Sal was often grumpy, but Beth could see he was a good man at heart.

Nellie was good to her. They'd sat together on the seat of the old pickup truck as Sal sat on the wooden bench he'd fashioned in the truck's engine compartment. As he steered the horses along the highways, the two got to know one another.

The old woman was confused, and thought young Beth was her granddaughter. Insisted on calling her Becky.

And although Beth was quick to argue with Sal about her name, she sensed a frailty in Nellie's mind. She didn't understand what Alzheimer's was, but she could tell the feeble old woman meant her no harm.

"Why," Sal asked Beth once, "do you let Nellie call you Becky without complaint, but you won't allow me to do the same?"

Beth took a deep breath before responding to him. As though she were a patient mother dealing with a petulant child.

"Because she doesn't know any better. It doesn't hurt to humor her. You, on the other hand, do know better. And besides, I want to keep my own identity for the day my daddy comes looking for me. If Nellie calls me Becky and you call me Becky, then I'm liable to forget who I really am."

"Honey, if I've told you once, I've told you a thousand times. Your daddy isn't coming to get you. Your family is dead. All of them. The man at the orphanage told me so."

In the end, they agreed to disagree about the whole adoption thing as well as the name.

Life at Benny's ranch wasn't lavish. But it was comfortable compared to the hardscrabble lives most of the other survivors were living. There was plenty to eat, other children to play with. Nellie and Sal seemed to love her, and Beth was growing fond of them.

And although Beth did have chores to do, so did everybody else.

All in all, her situation wasn't at all like her parents imagined. She was not being abused. She was not sold into slavery.

Although she missed her parents and often cried herself to sleep at night, hers was not a bad lot.

## Chapter 29

Beth did give one other concession to Nellie, in addition to answering when the old woman called her Becky.

She called her "Grandma."

It was awkward at first but Beth, who'd turned eight not long before, was a very wise child.

And she had a heart of gold.

She was in the corn field at Benny's place with Thom and Krista, eight and nine respectively. Thom and Krista were the children of the ranch's foreman, Bud Sykes.

Beth didn't particularly like Bud much. He was gruff and hairy and didn't bathe often. But his kids were always well groomed and manicured like their mother Mary.

And his children were nothing like Bud.

The three kids got along famously.

Except when it came to dealing with worms.

Corn husks are notorious for being infested with worms. There's nothing necessarily big and scary about them, but kids as a rule don't like worms much.

"Ewww!" Beth exclaimed as she reached up to pull off an ear and a snow white corn worm touched the back of her hand.

Then she stepped back two feet and did a little dance. It was the same dance eight year olds dance when they need to go to the restroom and there's not one close by.

"Thom, get it, get it!"

Even at eight years of age, little boys like to play the hero for little girls. And the truth was, the worms didn't bother him much. He'd gone through the cornfields on many occasions and gathered them up to use for fish bait.

They worked better than grub worms.

He reached up and plucked the little critter from the ear of corn, then held it up for Beth to see.

He'd saved the day. He was her knight in shining armor.

The truth was, Thom fancied little Beth.

Of course he was confused, as all the children were. Sal and Nellie called her Becky. She insisted her friends call her Beth.

"Except when you speak to Grandma Nellie. Then it's okay to call me Becky."

"Beth," Kristen asked as they walked through the rows to empty their bushel baskets. "How come they say you're an orphan?"

"Promise you'll keep it a secret," she told them, "and I'll tell you."

"But why keep it a secret? Are you ashamed of it?"

"No. Not at all. The truth is I'm not an orphan. I have a mommy and a sister who live somewhere near Kansas City, I think. With my Aunt Karen. I have a daddy too, but I haven't seen him since the blackout. Mommy says I have to keep believing, because he's coming to find us. But I don't know how in heck he's gonna find me now. *I* don't even know where we are."

"We're somewhere in California," Krista said. But if you have a mommy and a daddy, how come everybody says you're an orphan?"

"Because Sal got flimflammed, that's why."

"Sal got what?"

Beth liked it when she knew a fact or phrase that her peers did not know. It made her feel superior and a cut above them.

It made her feel *important.*

"That's something my daddy always says. It means the same thing as punked. Sal got flimflammed by Mr. Sanchez into thinking him and Grandma Nellie was adopting me, when actually he was buying me. Like a slave, and no darned better."

She almost said damned, but was afraid of getting her mouth washed out with soap.

Then it occurred to her that she was more intelligent than most kids her age. And that her mom was way too far away to wash her mouth out, with soap or anything else.

She believed her mom's promise that her daddy would come for her at some point. But since Sal and Nellie took her away and didn't tell her mommy where they were taking her, it might be awhile.

So she figured, what the heck.

"Sal was a damned fool for falling for that trick."

The other two stopped what they were doing and stared at her.

Thom's mouth dropped.

Krista demanded, "*What* did you say?"

Beth was incredibly proud of herself, and beamed.

"I said Sal was a damned fool for falling for Sanchez' dirty trick."

"You can't say that word. That's an adult word."

"I damned sure can."

Thom was aghast.

"She said it again."

Krista offered some older-child advice.

"You better stop using that word, Beth. You'll get into trouble."

"Oh, yeah? By who? My Mom is a zillion miles away. I don't know where my Dad is, but it's probably two zillion miles away. I'll probably be an old woman like Grandma Nellie before I see either one of them again. So who's gonna stop me if I say *damned* if I want to?"

Her logic gave pause to Krista, but only for a moment.

"I don't know. But that's an adult word. It's not nice for kids to say it."

"How come? How come adults are allowed to say words we can't? How come they're allowed to stay up as late as they want and we can't? How come they can eat all the candy and junk food they want but we can't?"

Thom finally found his tongue.

"Jeez, Beth, I don't know. That's just the way it is."

Beth suddenly felt powerful.

"Maybe it's time for a revolution."

"A what?"

"A revolution. That's when you're tired of something and you say enough is enough. My daddy told me about it. He said that one time they had a war about it or... something. I don't know. It's when you want to change stuff."

"What do you want to change, Beth? You're not making sense."

"I want to change everything. I want the kids to be in charge. I want us to be able to stay up all night and watch those movies that they say we can't watch. And I want to chew gum in my bed if I want to. And if it messes up my hair, I don't care. I'll cut it all off.

"And that's another thing. Who says I can't cut my own hair? I should be able to cut my own hair if I want."

Thom tried his best to help her cause.

"Krista cut her own bangs one time and it was a disaster."

Krista gave her brother the stink eye and said, "Shut up, stupid. It wasn't that bad."

"Was too."

Beth was losing her captive audience and wanted it back.

"Shut up you two. I say it's time we took charge of everything. We can tell Benny he's second in charge, but only if he does what we say. If he doesn't we'll fire him."

Thom shook his head, then pointed out the obvious.

"How are you gonna be brave enough to tell Benny that, when you're scared of a little ole worm?"

"Oh, shut up."

Thom looked across the yard to the farmhouse, where Benny was sitting on a lawn chair.

"Well, there's Benny right there, Miss Revolution. Why don't you go over there right now and tell him you're taking over?"

"I just might."

"Well, go ahead then."

Beth was in a corner she couldn't get out of. Her dad once told her never to let her mouth write checks her body couldn't cash.

She didn't have a clue what it meant. She should have listened a little better to his lesson.

She took a deep breath and stomped over to Benny, full of spit and vinegar and attitude.

"Mr. Benny!" she demanded.

Sal's brother turned and asked, "Yes, child. What is it?"

Something about the look on his kindly face forced the wind from her sails.

"Oh… nothing."

## Chapter 30

Dave tried to calm Tony's nerves. In no time at all he'd gone from considering Tony a soulless drug dealer to considering him a friend.

And they were partners now too, for better or for worse.

"Go ahead and make your map," Dave told him. "But I wouldn't worry much about them killing you. They need you too much. Or at least," he winked, "your drugs."

Tony replied glumly, "That's what keeps me alive when I go into the den with all the other lions. But Dalton's Raiders are a breed apart. Logic means nothing to them. When they get riled up, all common sense and logic goes right out the window."

"Don't give them any more credit than they're due. You'll be fine."

It had thundered a bit around the midnight hour, but didn't amount to much. Tony wiped a few drops of water from the seats of his ATV, and they were on the way.

They spoke nary a word as they rode due west, the rising sun warming their backs.

Each was lost in his own thoughts. Dave recalling over and over again the precious words from his wife and daughter. And wondering if this was the day he'd finally come face to face with little Beth and the monsters who'd stolen her.

Tony's silent thoughts were a bit more grim.

Tony's mother had the gift.

That's what the family called it: the gift. The ability to see glimpses of the future. To tell premonitions of things which were to happen.

It ran in the family. Tony's mom had it, and his grandmother too. It was said that his great-grandmother foretold her own death.

When Tony was five his mother suddenly cancelled a planned vacation. They were to stay with friends at a resort in Savannah, Georgia.

"Something bad's going to happen," she said. But she didn't elaborate. Couldn't elaborate. She knew none of the details, only a feeling of doom.

She begged out of the event, and tried to talk their friends into cancelling as well. But they scoffed at her. Called her foolish and hinted she'd been nipping at the bottle.

Three of her friends perished when the resort caught fire at three in the morning.

Tony occasionally had premonitions as well. Sometimes they came true. As often as not, though, they weren't even close.

By the law of averages, he reasoned, the ones which came true were more than likely just coincidences.

The night before, as he was trying to sleep, he had a vision of his boys crying.

He'd been trying for months to get through to them via the ham. But in his vision, they were calling for him.

And when he heard his wife's voice coming over the airwaves, it wasn't Tony who answered. It was Dave.

The words were chilling and unmistakable.

"I'm sorry. Tony went to visit some very bad men. And they slaughtered him."

*Slaughtered.* Who in hell talked like that? And who in hell would use the phrase to tell a grieving wife her husband had been murdered?

Tony had been as upset about Dave's choice of words as in his own death.

He tried to laugh it off. After all, he'd been wrong so many times before.

He'd be wrong this time as well. And later, when the two relaxed at his home on the eastern part of town, he'd laugh and admit his folly to Dave. Dave would likely tell him he was nuts. He'd likely lecture him that with

Dave having his back, there was no need for such silly worries. Or sillier premonitions.

"Nothing's going to happen to you," he'd say. "As long as I have your six, you'll live forever."

## Chapter 31

At mile marker 156 Tony pulled next to a Walmart rig with what looked like a mountain of trash piled behind it.

In reality, it was a pile of perfectly good merchandize from the truck which wasn't deemed vital for survival and was in the way of other items. So it was thrown unceremoniously out the door of the trailer by a series of looters.

In that regard, it looked just like hundreds of other tractor trailer rigs which spotted the interstate highways.

This particular trailer would be Dave's home for the next couple or three hours.

"I'm going to drop you off here. Take the time to root through the trailer, See if you can find anything of value, though you can bet all the water and most of the food is gone by now."

"That's okay, I brought my own."

Tony wouldn't let him bring any weapons. Tony was a firm believer that carrying weapons could make a dangerous mission more dangerous by aggravating the situation. It was one of the few things they disagreed on.

So Dave's backpack held no weapons. But it did hold seven bottles of water and four cans of Campbell's Chunky soup. His favorite flavor, clam chowder.

He had no place to heat it up, of course, but it was good cold, out of the can.

He'd manage.

Tony pulled out the map he'd drawn the night before and showed it to his partner.

"Okay, take a minute to look this over, make sure it makes sense to you."

He pointed out landmarks on the map with his finger as he explained.

"I'm not sure of the house number, but it's on Baker Street about a mile north and west of the checkpoint. To get there, go due north past the checkpoint until you get to a Valero convenience store. Then head west. Turn north again at a boarded up gas station, and it's about three blocks up. Not far at all.

"The house is directly across the street from an elementary school, on the corner. It's brick, one story, with a Ford van parked in the driveway. A blue one.

"You can't miss it because the side of the house is spray painted in yellow paint with the words, "Dalton's Raiders rule the world."

"Subtle."

"Yeah."

"Think you can find it?"

"Piece of cake."

Tony checked his watch.

"Okay, it's almost noon. I should be out by three. If they're in a mood to visit, it might take a bit longer.

"If I'm not out by five, something's wrong. They're either holding me against my will or I'm dead."

"Tony, I want you to be honest with me. Is your going in there and asking about the red pickup going to put your life in danger? Because if it is I'll leave you out of it and I'll go in alone."

"Honestly, Dave, going in there for any reason is dangerous. I've thought many times about just cutting off my business with the Dalton people and cutting my losses. Except if I did that, they're crazy enough to put out a hit on me and send people looking for me.

"So no, asking about your red pickup won't make a dangerous situation any more so. If anything, it'll help the situation. Their booze supply, like everyone else's, has been running short. The news that I'll be bringing some in may brighten their spirits a bit."

There wasn't much left to be said.

Dave said, "Good luck, my friend."

Tony got the strangest look on his face.

"What? You don't want me to wish you luck?"

"No. It's not that. It's just that you called me a friend. And it occurred to me you're probably the only one. I have a lot of acquaintances. I know a lot of people. But they're not my friends. They all want something from me. Or I pay them to guard my house or the dope I have stashed here and there. But I don't think I've had a friend since... for awhile."

"What can I say, Tony? We started out with a business relationship, then became partners. Now you're a friend. I guess you've just grown on me, like toenail fungus or something."

Tony smiled.

"Good luck to you too. And while I don't believe in your God, if you have a desire to do so, say a little prayer for me, okay?"

"Ha! I knew it. You are a believer. You just don't like to admit it."

Tony turned away and drove off, leaving Dave's question unanswered.

Dave looked toward the sky and said, "God, please look after that little guy. He's got his faults, like we all do. But he's got a good heart and he's a good man."

Dave hadn't slept well the night before. He was exhausted from having spent too many hours in the dead of night, staring at the ceiling and thinking about the words his wife and daughter had told him.

And wondering about little Beth. Whether she was alive or dead. Whether she was being treated well. He knew that even slave owners in the old days usually didn't overwork their slaves. Their lives were brutal, but slave owners knew they couldn't work if they didn't stay healthy.

He hoped that wherever Beth was, she was well fed and given ample chance to rest.

He didn't know what the future held for any of them, but he knew what his short term plans were.

He was going to try to take a nap. He had at least three hours before Tony was due back.

And there didn't seem to be much else to do.

He climbed aboard the Walmart trailer and began picking through what was left on it.

On one of the pallets close to the front of the trailer he found a case of blow-up air mattresses. The case had been opened and several had been taken out.

But there were three left.

"Jackpot!"

It took him several minutes to blow up the mattress. And several more to decide on a place to nap. He finally settled on a spot beneath the huge trailer. It seemed to be ant-free and shaded from the sun, which was now high in the sky.

He fell asleep almost as soon as he lay down.

## Chapter 32

Dave was awakened by two men walking past the trailer and carrying on a heated conversation. Apparently one was accusing the other of eating more than his share of... something. The first was denying the charge and leveling his own countercharges.

Before he even opened his eyes, Dave was reaching for a weapon beneath his pillow.

It was a survival technique he'd developed since the blackout. One he'd honed to the point it came automatically, without thinking, any time he was disturbed from his sleep. And perhaps he'd moved just a tiny bit faster in this instance because his subconscious detected a hostile tone in the passing voices.

The problem was, Dave had no weapon.

He didn't even have a pillow.

And he felt naked and vulnerable.

He should never have given in to Tony's insistence they move about the city unarmed.

To Tony, being unarmed was an assurance to the factions he dealt with on a daily basis that he was no threat to them. That he was merely a merchant selling his wares.

To Dave, not having a weapon in the new post-blackout world was just stupid.

To Dave, guns were tools. Perhaps the greatest tool man ever invented.

A wrench could remove a bolt. And that was all well and good. But a gun could help remove a threat.

Bolts couldn't kill you. Threats could.

As the men continued walking down the highway and the threat passed, Dave made a mental note to bring up the subject again with Tony. And to offer his friend some weapons training. Perhaps if he was proficient in the use of firearms he'd be more accepting of them.

He checked his watch. It was just past two p.m. Had he really been out for two hours?

Dave listened for the now-familiar roar of Tony's Polaris. He said he expected to be back by three. It shouldn't be long now.

He used the tail of the black t-shirt he wore to wipe the sweat from his face. Two o'clock typically marked the highest temperature of any day, and he figured it to be in the low 90s.

If the passing men hadn't awakened him, his sweating soon would have.

He rolled off the air mattress and from beneath the trailer, then stood on the shoulder of the road.

His back was cramping again and it occurred to him he was getting old.

No, maybe not. But he had a lot more aches and pains than he once did. Perhaps his new harsh life, living on the road, was taking a toll on his body. And he wondered how bad it would be ten or twenty years from now.

Then he banished the thought from his mind, as being too disheartening to think about.

Once upon a time he walked into the woods when he needed to relieve himself.

Now, though, people no longer saw the need to be discrete. Relieving oneself in public had become socially acceptable, and the call of nature was no longer necessarily kept private.

Well, among men, anyway. Most women still liked to cling to old societal norms, and preferred to urinate in more private confines than the open road.

Men these days tended to just whip it out and let loose, wherever they happened to be at the time, without regard to who might be in the close vicinity.

As Dave peed against the front wheel of the GMC tractor it occurred to him that he'd adopted a habit he needed to shed before he found little Beth. It didn't matter that most other men did the same thing.

They weren't Beth's father.

Dave was, and as such needed to set a better example.

He resolved, when he was finished, that in the future he'd do it the old way. The way he did when he first hit the road and struck out from San Antonio.

God, that seemed so long ago.

In the future, he'd do what he used to do, and seek out a stand of bushes to hide in when he needed to use the restroom.

Or, in an urban setting, he'd go behind a building or other structure.

It had been well over a year since the EMPs struck the earth out of the blue and did their damage.

For well over a year, Dave hadn't had to use courtesy or manners or etiquette to get by. He'd lived alone during that time and behaved more or less the way he wanted to.

He didn't have to fill his role as a father, or to set an example for his daughters, because they were a thousand miles away.

He wasn't sure where Beth was. She might be only a couple of miles from him at that very moment.

One thing he was sure of, though, was that he'd soon find her. He'd soon go back to being her daddy, and the one she looked to for protection and guidance.

In advance of that, he resolved that he'd rid himself of some of his bad habits.

He climbed back onto the trailer and was surprised to find there were a few cases of water left, although most had been removed from the pallet.

One case had been torn open, and he helped himself to six bottles.

Then he got the heck out of the trailer, as the afternoon sun had heated it to well over a hundred degrees.

The six bottles of water were also way too hot to drink. But that was no problem.

He placed them into his backpack and would drink them later after they'd cooled off. He took out two other bottles, cooler ones, from the bowels of the pack.

Dave took three large swallows from one of the bottles, then used an old Marine Corps trick to try to get his core temperature down a bit.

He took off the black t-shirt he wore and soaked it with the rest of the water in the bottle.

Once the shirt was soaked through and through he held his breath and put it back on.

It was always a shock when the wet shirt hit his chest and back. But the shock dissipated after a few seconds. And for the next two hours or so, until the shirt dried again, he'd be the coolest guy in the neighborhood.

## Chapter 33

By four thirty Dave was starting to worry. He'd served two combat tours in Iraq. He knew that, despite the military's wishes, campaigns sometimes didn't go according to plan.

Sometimes unexpected obstacles jumped up and got in the way.

Sometimes the enemy combatants didn't behave as expected.

Sometimes enemy reinforcements showed up and had to be dealt with.

Sometimes miscalculations were made.

And sometimes timetables weren't met.

The concept that all operations in the United States Marine Corps were timed and conducted with precision, right down to the minute, was a myth.

Especially during combat.

Oh, a campaign might start dead on a pre-planned minute.

But after that, anything was possible.

The difference between a campaign the Marines were running in Fallujah, and the mission Tony was on in Albuquerque, was that the Marines were in constant contact with each other.

They could communicate by radio to let each other know as plans changed, as new threats emerged.

And, if comm was out, they could use runners or even colored smoke grenades to send coded messages back and forth.

The mission Tony was on was amateur by comparison.

Dave understood that odds were Tony merely let time get away from him. And he'd mentioned something about the Dalton gang keeping him longer than he wanted to be there to socialize.

Dave had gotten the impression from Tony that if the gang wanted to visit, one didn't have the option of saying no.

And knowing that military excursions into enemy territory seldom if ever went as planned, Dave tried his best not to worry.

But now it was sixteen thirty hours. Tony said he should be back at fifteen hundred. He was an hour and a half late.

It was hard *not* to worry.

His t-shirt was almost dry now and he was getting uncomfortably hot again. He thought about re-wetting it, but looked for the tenth time at the southern sky.

A storm front was building to the south and the skies were darkening.

And it appeared to be headed his way.

Dave didn't particularly like the idea of riding back to Tony's place on Tony's ATV, a driving rain in their faces.

But at least it would cool things off.

The storm looked to be an hour or so away. He could tough out the heat until then, and chose not to waste water to soak his shirt again.

He hated idle time. Always had.

If he had a rifle, he could shoot the good sized rabbit eating grass on the opposite side of the highway.

If he had his fishing gear, he could hike down to a small playa lake a hundred yards away to see if there were any fish in it.

If it wasn't so damn hot inside the trailer, he'd crawl back inside and rummage through the leftovers to see whether there was anything left worth taking.

He was limited to three options while he waited: he could eat.

Or he could try to doze off again, but he knew he wouldn't be able to. His stress level was rising ever higher as each minute went by with no sign of Tony.

The third option was to worry.

But he knew he'd do that anyway, regardless of whether he was lying down or eating.

So he might as well eat.

And that made good sense anyway. For if they were holding Tony against his will, and he had to go to war later to rescue him, Dave would need his strength. And he probably wouldn't be able to eat later.

In battlefield etiquette, it was extremely bad form to hold up one's hand and say, "Time out, I need to eat."

And probably a little bit dangerous as well.

## Chapter 34

Dave climbed over the door of a Mustang convertible and sat in the passenger seat while popping the lid off a can of clam chowder.

He always used disposable plastic spoons when he ate canned food. That way he didn't have to wash his utensils. And the plastic dinnerware was easy to find. It was all over the place, in pretty much every Walmart trailer he'd ever crawled into.

Especially the knives. Highway nomads frequently helped themselves to the forks and spoons for their own use.

But nobody ever took the knives.

As he ate the cold clam chowder, Dave envisioned a world five years in the future, when virtually everything of value had been liberated from such trailers. And in his vision of the future, only two things would be left, scattered about the floor of each trailer:

Plastic knives and kitty litter.

To occupy his thoughts and reduce his stress level Dave looked around the interior of the Mustang. The top had been opened when it died more than a year before, and it had suffered extensive water damage from passing rains. And even more damage from the sun.

But it was still in surprisingly good shape.

It reminded him that he'd always wanted a Mustang convertible.

His parents wouldn't let him buy one in high school because... well, they knew him too well. They knew he had a lead foot and would show off to his friends.

They knew him as a rather inattentive driver as well, distracted by every pretty girl in a skirt walking down the street.

If he'd succeeded in talking them into the convertible, his parents feared he'd eventually wrap the car around a tree.

And they were rather fond of their only son, so they told him no.

After high school he still wanted one, but couldn't afford it. College was taking pretty much all of his money, barely leaving him enough money for a ramen noodle diet.

Still, he had to get to and from classes. So he took a second job until he scraped together enough for a 1963 Ford Galaxie 500.

It was a Ford. It was a well-built, if not so attractive machine.

But it wasn't a Mustang convertible.

Dave finished his clam chowder and said what the heck. He opened up the second can and ate that too. If he were going to war later in the day he might not be able to stop and eat again for awhile.

And besides, going into battle with less weight to carry on his back was always a positive thing.

Dave was good at rationalization. At making excuses to justify doing things he wanted to do anyway.

The truth was he ate the second can simply because he liked the taste of the first one so much he wanted more.

By the time he finished the second can, Tony was way overdue.

Dave tried to keep calm. He was well aware that wartime missions frequently took longer than expected.

And make no mistake about it.

Tony had gone into a heavily armed camp. Full of hostiles with a bloodlust and a tendency to kill first and ask questions later. A group who frequently killed even those they should have considered friends.

They were thousands of miles from Fallujah. But Dave recognized this was as difficult and dangerous a mission for Tony as Dave ever went on.

And he was two hours late.

Dave tried his best not to worry. But it was getting harder and harder as each minute went by.

He tried to occupy his mind, not with thoughts of what might have gone wrong. But of more pleasant thoughts.

He climbed out of the Mustang, careful to place the two empty soup cans upright on the floorboard so they didn't soil the seats.

Like it mattered.

But hey, it was a Mustang convertible.

He popped the hood and suddenly remembered the joy of working on a car in simpler times.

This was a 1970 model. A classic. It was manufactured at a time before cars became mostly plastic. It was heavier, with a very powerful engine that drank gas like it was water, but by God, it was built to last.

He looked down at each side of the Boss 302 engine and could see the ground beneath the car.

This car was built in the days before the EPA required a myriad of vacuum hoses and catalytic converters and emissions control crap that weighed the cars down and made it impossible to crawl into an engine compartment and become one with the engine.

It was simple, it was fast, and it was easy to work on.

In a single word, it was beautiful.

Oddly enough, he could still smell the burned wiring that was so potent as it permeated the air on the day the EMPs struck. It came wafting out at him when he opened the hood, as though he needed any reminder of the hell the EMPs had brought upon the earth and its people.

He looked at each of the vital components, wondering what it would take to make this beast run again. It was folly, and he knew it. For even if it could be repaired, he had no time to look for parts or try to overhaul them. And even if he did get it running, he couldn't drive two vehicles at the same time. And the Explorer was much more suited to his needs.

The battery was fried, that was obvious. The positive cable was melted to the point the plastic covering had dripped into a gooey red mess which still adorned the pavement beneath the battery.

The starter was equally destroyed. He could tell because its outer casing was blackened with soot at the ventilation ports.

The alternator appeared to have survived.

There was no electronic ignition, not back in 1970. No electronic fuel injection system either.

Surely the fuses were all blown, the wiring for the lights and wipers and other stuff probably worthless.

But Dave wondered if he found a new starter at an auto parts store somewhere, and was able to replace the battery, whether he could get this old girl running again.

It was a nice thought and a pleasant way to get his mind off the situation at hand.

But enough was enough.

He had far more important things to think about.

## Chapter 35

Tony had told him that if he wasn't back by five, something was wrong. It took all the strength Dave could muster, but he dutifully waited.

Now it was five o'clock. Seventeen hundred hours.

Time to head out.

As he walked at a brisk pace toward the part of the city Tony called "Crazy Town," Dave cursed under his breath.

He was going into battle naked. No weapons at all, thanks to Tony's insane assistance that guns were dangerous.

It was something he and Tony would never agree on, even if they were friends and partners for a thousand years.

A gun in the hands of someone who knew how to use it was dangerous, sure. But only for the men who would challenge him. And they deserved no quarter if they were posing a threat to him.

A gun in the hands of the good guys wasn't just smart, it was necessary.

Ordinarily Dave wouldn't have let anyone talk him into giving up his weapons. Not even temporarily.

But Tony had been adamant. He'd agreed to help Dave only under his own rules. In his estimation, going in unarmed was a better and safer tactic.

Dave ceded that Tony knew the men they were dealing with better than he did. Perhaps there was an unwritten rule Dave didn't know about which said that visitors who showed up armed were shot on sight.

And indeed, the Crips and the MS-13 sentries both insisted on patting Dave and Tony down.

Still, Dave had wondered whether there was more to Tony's point of view than met the eye.

In his experience, strict anti-gun people usually had a story to tell. A little brother shot and killed himself because some fool left a loaded weapon within his reach. Or a parent was shot and killed by an armed robber. Or... something.

Most of the anti-gun people Dave had met over the years had a reason they were so anti-gun. Perhaps Tony had his own reason. Dave had never gotten around to asking, and Tony wasn't exactly a man who was forthcoming about his personal life.

It was a question which had gone unanswered and now Dave kicked himself for not prying a bit more. If Tony had an innate fear of guns because of something which happened in his past, Dave could have addressed it.

Dave could have explained that guns don't just take lives. That far more often, in the right hands, they save them. They can be the most valuable tool ever invented for protecting a man's loved ones and property.

And in a case of kill or be killed, it's the man with the gun who'll win out over the man armed only with words.

Every single time.

Yet Dave let himself he disarmed, even though he knew better. He hadn't expected to like Tony. Going in he expected Tony to be just another drug dealer bent on infecting as many people as possible with the scourge of addiction. Just to maximum his profits.

But Tony was more than that. Tony showed Dave that it was possible for a drug dealer to be a decent human being. Maybe it was a contradiction. But Dave was convinced Tony was more good than evil.

Dave had been swayed because he yielded to Tony's experience in dealing with the people they had to deal with.

And Tony's assurances they'd have much better success going in under the factions' terms.

After all, it boiled down to needs.

Dave *needed* Tony's help to go in and find the red pickup.

Tony *needed* the factions' help to help find the pickup.

So against his better judgment, Dave allowed himself to be swayed.

Now he had to go into the lion's den with no weapons at all. Most of his weapons were in a canvas Army mobility bag, hidden next to a dumpster beneath a mountain of garbage some twelve miles east of them.

Even his sidearm and AR-15 were in the bag.

He was in a hell of a pickle.

He shouldn't have given up his guns.

## Chapter 36

Dave's first excursion into the enemy's camp would be a recon mission. If he came across any weapons and ammunition he could easily liberate and use for his own benefit he'd do so.

But that wasn't very likely.

He'd have to assume his only weapons would be his bare hands and his head.

And his head, of course, was what allowed him to be placed in this predicament to begin with.

He should have argued with Tony to at least let him bring his AR and sidearm that morning. Not to take into Crazy Town, but to keep with him.

Just in case he had to go in.

Dave would go in, even without arms.

He had to. His partner was in there.

And Dave was Corps through and through.

You didn't leave a man behind. You just didn't.

By the time Dave made it the mile to the exit Tony had marked on his map, the sun was getting low in the sky.

He used it to his advantage.

He saw the sentries at the Dalton's Raiders camp as he walked by them, behind a spray painted Lincoln Town Car. They eyed him suspiciously as he walked past, but didn't challenge him.

He looked just like dozens of others who walked down the interstate each and every day.

He continued west on the interstate another quarter mile or so, then waited behind an abandoned cement mixer.

Now came the tricky part.

The sun would be setting in just a few minutes. When it did so, he'd be hidden from view to the sentries east of him. If they happened to look to the west, they'd get an eyeful. But it wouldn't be of Dave. It would be of the blinding sun.

The area west of Dave was a different matter.

If there were any sentries to the west of him, they'd be able to see Dave easily.

Tactics weren't enough in this case. Dave would require a healthy dose of luck as well, to pull this off.

Luckily the service road just below the interstate was heavily clogged with abandoned cars. With any luck he could dart from car to car, using them as shields, until he cleared the service road and disappeared into the residential neighborhood just on the other side of it.

He kept an eye on the sun, and when it half disappeared below the horizon he held his breath and ran low to the first vehicle on the service road.

It was a Ford 150 pickup truck, and he kept it on his left shoulder as he waited for gunshots or shouting.

Instead he heard silence.

Of course, it was possible there was silence because he was spotted and the sentries were lining up their shots.

They had to know he'd be moving to the next car on the service road momentarily.

They might, at that very moment, be lining up their shots in the gap between that next car and the pickup he was hiding behind.

He hoped not. But he'd soon find out for certain.

He held his breath again and sprinted over the fifteen yard gap to the next car.

A blue Hyundai.

His luck was still holding. There were no gunshots, no yelling, no indications at all he'd been spotted.

The next gap was even longer. It was an all out forty yard sprint across somebody's front yard to the alley behind their house.

This was where he'd be shot, if it was going to happen. For there was simply nothing substantial to give him cover between the Hyundai and the alley. A few shrubs which might help hide him.

But they'd certainly stop no bullet.

If anyone had eyes on him he was dead meat.

Then he had an epiphany.

It would be dark in just a few minutes.

He felt like an idiot.

Then he lay down, hidden from both sides east and west, trying to ponder his next move.

The only problem was, he didn't have one.

He had the map to Dalton's headquarters, sure.

But a fat lot of good it did him.

Once he got there, then what? What if Tony wasn't there? What if he was waylaid while making his deliveries and robbed of his drugs and his ATV? The confines of Crazy Town, Tony had told him, encompassed almost ten square miles.

If he was being held in one of those houses, Dave would have a hell of a time figuring out which one. If he was beaten and left bleeding in some alley, Dave would have to determine which one of hundreds of such alleys.

And what if he was still at Dalton's HQ, bound and gagged and being held for... who knew what? To hear Tony tell it, Dalton and his henchmen needed no reason to conduct the chaos they dealt... only a time and a place to do it.

If he found Tony in such a situation, Dave doubted very seriously the Dalton gang would cotton to him just waltzing in and saying "Hi fellas. How ya doin'? I'm just gonna untie my friend and take him home now."

It was possible, considering how crazy they were.

But highly unlikely.

No. This first mission would be a recon mission.

He'd use it to gather information only, unless he happened upon an unguarded weapons cache.

He'd try his best to determine Tony's location, present condition and circumstances. Whether he was wounded in some way. Whether he was incapacitated. Whether he was tied up and being held against his will.

If that was the case, Dave would try to ascertain what their motives were. If they even had a motive.

Also, what the enemy's troop strength was. Where they were posted. What time they changed shifts.

Most of all he'd look for weak spots. Things he could exploit.

Then and only then would he make the day-long journey back to the trash pile to get his weapons.

It seemed dark enough to go now.

He looked in all directions, wishing like hell he still had his night vision goggles.

And he stole away down the nearest alley.

## Chapter 37

Dave worked his way slowly through the alleys running adjacent to the street on his map. Since Tony used landmarks instead of street names, he had to peer out each time he came to a cross street to see whether there was a Valero on the street corner.

Once he found the Valero, he headed west. This time there was no alley to take cover in, so the going was much slower. He darted from bush to bush, from abandoned car to abandoned car.

At one point he ducked behind a house so he could use his cigarette lighter to check his map.

The night was disorienting, and he couldn't afford to get lost.

Finally, he reached the boarded up gas station he was looking for, and headed north again

The storm front finally hit at that point and the skies opened up.

"Gee, thanks," Dave muttered while looking toward the sky. "I really could have used you when I had to sneak across that damn highway."

But it was what it was.

It was a while in coming, but since the rain was finally there he'd use it as an ally.

He knew that the rain in conjunction with the dark of night would make it much more difficult for sentries to see Dave coming.

In his estimation, he could probably stroll leisurely down the middle of the street and not be spotted by the houses on either side of it.

Not that he was going to try it.

In any event, the comfort of knowing he couldn't be seen didn't last long.

When Dave was in an open area between two abandoned cars a flash of lightning almost directly overhead illuminated the whole area.

"Shit!"

He'd told himself he was going to stop using that word, since he expected to find and liberate Beth very soon, and would have her by his side.

But no other word in his vocabulary seemed to apply.

He dove to the ground until the skies darkened again.

Exactly three blocks north from the boarded up gas station Tony came to an intersection and waited until another lightning flash.

Hiding in the bushes against the corner house, he patiently sat, talking to the gods of the sky once again.

"Okay, now, help me out. I can't see a damn thing out there."

As he waited he thought he caught the putrid scent of burned human flesh. But he quickly dismissed it. The burning of bodies had become a routine thing in every urban setting in America. It was quicker and easier than burials.

The sky flashed brightly again for a couple of seconds.

Just long enough for Dave to make out a deserted elementary school on the opposite corner to his left.

And directly across the street from him, on a brick house, he just barely made out graffiti in fluorescent yellow spray paint.

"Dalton's Raiders Rule The World."

Jackpot.

Tony was a hell of a mapmaker.

He was elated. The first and most critical step in tonight's mission was to find his enemy. Nothing else could be done until he succeeded at that. No intel gathering, no rescue. Nothing.

So he was one big step closer in accomplishing the night's mission.

He waited in place for the next lightning flash, wishing he had some binoculars.

Until he moved closer, onto the actual property, his movements would be guided solely by the occasional lighting of the sky. For he still had to ascertain for certain the threat he faced.

Suddenly lightning filled the sky, just long enough for Dave to see there was no one on the porch of the house before him.

That struck him as odd. Surely their security people must know they were especially vulnerable at night. And doubly so when it rained at night.

Obviously Tony was right. This wasn't your typical group of thugs.

On the next lighting flash Dave looked closely at the shrubbery against the front of the house and below the picture window. The shrubs were empty, the drapes were closed.

It was time to go.

But no.

For in the last millisecond of light, before the flash of lightning ran its course, Dave thought he saw something out of the corner of his eye.

Something in the street, between the house in front of him, and the blackened hulk of the abandoned school.

Something which looked very much like... a crumpled human body.

He waited some fifteen seconds, until the next flash confirmed his suspicions.

And for every one of those fifteen seconds he prayed a silent prayer.

Which did not come true.

He fairly ran to the spot, even while knowing he was exposing himself in the process.

He went to one knee beside Tony, who'd been doused with gasoline and burned alive while the lunatics danced around him.

Tony had screamed and rolled as best he could. But his hands and feet, bound with leather belts, had limited his movements.

His tormentors had laughed at him, comparing him to a fish out of water, flopping around in his last moments.

But Tony was stubborn, and much tougher than they gave him credit for.

He hadn't died.

Oh, he stopped moving after a couple of agonizing minutes.

His heartbeat slowed to next to nothing. His breathing went shallow.

But he wasn't dead. He mercifully passed out and slipped into unconsciousness. It was his brain's way of dealing with pain he could not handle.

When his body went limp, the flames lapped off the remaining bits of clothing until he was pretty much naked in the street.

At the same time the raindrops started to fall, cooling his body and making steam rise from it.

The steam, the rain, the horrible stench combined to make a desperately sadistic act seem almost surreal.

Or maybe *macabre* would be the best word.

Dave was sure he was dead.

As he felt for a pulse, he demanded of the crumpled figure, "Why? Why did they have to do this to you?"

He heard a moan.

It was so faint he wasn't even sure it was real. The rain had slowed to a trickle, though, and he heard it again.

He felt no pulse. The blood pressure was too low, the heart was barely beating.

But he knew dead men didn't moan.

He rolled Tony onto his back and placed his face next to his friend's.

"Tony," he said. "I'm here. As God is my witness I will avenge you.

Tony struggled to open his eyes. He wanted to look at his friend one last time before he passed.

But his eyelids were fused to his eyeballs. They'd never open again.

"I can't... I can't feel anything, Dave. Shouldn't I be burning or something?"

Dave had seen similar injuries in Iraq. Tony was beyond hope. Dave couldn't save him. He was very close to death.

The least he could do was to be straight with him. To not mislead him.

"Your nervous system has shut down. It's taken away your pain."

He coughed.

"Dave, listen to me. They never made it inside. The sentries laughed at them and sent them away. They told the old man his pickup truck looked ridiculous pulled by two broken down old horses. The last time they were seen they were headed west on the interstate away from the city."

Dave was stunned. In his final act on earth, Tony had been doing Dave's work. He not only accomplished his mission, he'd accomplished Dave's as well. And now he was dying and Dave couldn't do a damn thing about it. Tony was too far gone and they both knew it.

Even in the old days, when ambulances still worked and trauma centers were fully staffed and operational, he wouldn't have made it.

"Dave," he wheezed. "Don't avenge me. My luck finally ran out. I knew it would eventually. Go get your daughter. She needs you more than I do."

He never exhaled. He expended all of his final breath with his last words. His body merely went limp.

And it occurred to Dave he never even said thank you.

Dave was stunned. So much so that he sat in the middle of that street, unarmed and totally vulnerable, for several more minutes.

Cradling his friend's head in his lap.

Wishing he could speak to him just a bit more.

Every time the lightning flashed he could have been spotted. Could have been shot.

But he wasn't.

And by not shooting him when they had several chances to do so, the animals in the Dalton house sealed their own fate.

## Chapter 38

Dave felt bad that he hadn't thanked his friend. Hadn't prayed for him before he died. Tony might have objected anyway, given his claims of being a non-believer.

Dave really did believe the old adage that there were no atheists in foxholes. Men who neared death almost always hedged their bets by praying, even to a God they professed not to believe in.

He thought Tony might have found some comfort in hearing Dave's words, asking God to take him under His wings and to watch over him.

But Dave didn't do that either. He was caught up in the moment, trying to wrap his arms around it all. The realization he'd lost a friend. The knowledge Beth wasn't even in Albuquerque. And that meant the odds of her being alive were so much greater. The fact he'd soon be leaving the city confines to begin his search anew.

He was a jumble of emotions. Sadness, elation, regret.

Tony was gone now. He was in no more pain. He was at peace. And surely God would recognize his last act was one of kindness, and would forgive him for all that non-believer stuff.

Just in case, Dave bent his head. The rain picked up again and rolled in a tiny torrent off the point of his chin as he prayed aloud on Tony's behalf.

He couldn't bury his friend under the circumstances. He couldn't burn him either. So he did the next best thing.

He carried Tony to a tree in the front yard of the Dalton house and placed him under it.

"Rest in Peace, my friend. They will pay for what they've done to you."

He looked to the house, still incredulous that no one was standing guard. No one was peering through the windows.

No one seemed to care.

He walked up the steps and onto the porch. A particularly bold move in light of the fact he had no way to defend himself.

It was a reckless and stupid act. Had he been in a better frame of mind, he'd have stolen away in the dead of the night and regrouped. Come back at a later time when he was more level headed and more prepared.

But on this particular night he wasn't himself.

He was in a rage and bent on sending these men to hell.

There was a party atmosphere within the house. He smelled the pungent aroma of marijuana smoke. It surely was Tony's, for he'd claimed he was the only supplier who had the guts to come into such a sewer.

He wondered if that was why they'd killed him. Had they merely wanted his drugs and didn't want to pay for them? Then why not take them and just let him ride away?

Tony had said they were unstable. That their actions defied reason. He'd said they just did what they did without regard to reasoning.

Had they killed him just because they needed something to do?

The heavy drapes had been drawn, but there were gaps Dave could peek through. The interior of the house was lighted with electric lamps, which meant there was a generator running in the backyard.

And although he needed no more reason to hate these men, his hatred grew as he looked into the window.

Three men were huddled around a water pipe, smoking marijuana. Two others were smoking crystal meth from a glass oil burner, passing it back and forth between them.

Yet another was forming lines of coke atop a coffee table.

And all of them... every damn one of them, was laughing and carrying on as though it were a frat party.

It was all Dave could do to keep from crashing through the window and strangling as many as he could with his bare hands, until someone found the presence of mind to shoot him.

But that wouldn't help him get to Beth or get her back. All it would do is condemn her to a lifetime of slavery.

He'd seen Tony's Polaris parked haphazardly against the porch. Its black and woodland camouflage paint scheme helped it blend in well into the shadows, but the occasional lightning flash lit it up like a Christmas tree.

He walked over to it to see whether the key was still in the ignition.

It shouldn't have surprised him that it was. But then again, who in their right mind would steal from a group of insane blood-lusted men who killed without reason even those they needed?

He climbed aboard the machine and brought it to life.

"I'll be back, you bastards."

## Chapter 40

Dave already knew that a Polaris, creeping along at its own pace with no foot on the accelerator, made virtually no sound at all.

Other than the sound the pavement made as the balloon tires rolled over it.

The pouring rain deadened even that sound, and the machine moved as quietly as a whisper.

Still, just to be safe, he stayed off the streets and took the same route he'd come in on, through the alleys.

One thing he didn't know was whether the Dalton gang had working radios. The fact that they had a working generator and working lights certainly made that possible. If they either had a prepper in their employ or had robbed one of his goodies, they might well have a base station as well as handhelds.

If they had such gear, and if they'd heard him start the Polaris and drive off on it, there was a good chance the sentries at the highway on-ramp were already watching for him.

He fully expected to have to abandon the ATV when he got to the service road and hoof it from car to car, the same way he'd gotten in.

But then again, maybe not.

The storm was getting heavier, the visibility getting worse.

Dark rain clouds covered the partial moon and stars. It was damn near pitch black.

That was the good news.

The bad news was, between the heavy rain and the darkness it was getting harder and harder to see what was in front of him.

As he left the house headed back to the highway he weighed his options. There were three. First, he could play it safe and ditch the Polaris, go out the way he came in, and avoid the sentries and their checkpoint altogether.

Or he could try to creep silently past them, assuming they'd take refuge in the Lincoln Town Car. He was pretty sure he could get by them, waiting until he got to the highway to pick up his speed.

The third and last option was merely to gun and run, trying to speed his way past the checkpoint. Catch them with their pants down, so to speak, and try to get past them before they recovered enough to shoot at him. And knowing they'd have little chance of hitting him, firing blindly into the dark night and a driving rain.

The third option was out now. He couldn't speed anywhere. There were cars all over the place he could no longer see.

Not until he crashed into them, anyway. And crashing the Polaris anywhere near the sentries wouldn't play well for him.

That left two choices. And he didn't want to abandon the Polaris, simply because he didn't want to have to walk the twelve miles back to his weapons. That was an all day hike even in dry weather. If the storms continued it would stretch into two full days.

No. He had to drive the Polaris out of the camp. He'd need it.

He drove as quickly as he dared toward the checkpoint, and parked the ATV fifty yards away. He left it there and moved carefully from one shadowy silhouette of a vehicle to the next, until he was mere yards from the Town Car.

The sentries were inside, the windows all fogged up from their body heat.

Under other circumstances Dave would have surely smiled. He might have even laughed out loud. The so-called sentries, the ones Dalton counted on to provide security and prevent hostile enemies from entering their compound, chose comfort over doing their jobs.

They couldn't have seen a semi drive by with its headlights on high beams.

Yes, under other circumstances Dave might have laughed.

But tonight he just didn't feel like it.

He jogged back to the Polaris and fumbled around in the dark trying to find the ignition.

A lightning bolt directly overhead took mercy on him and gave him enough light to see the keyhole. The same bolt flashed long enough to give him an idea what lay ahead of him for the next hundred yards or so.

He committed it to memory while he waited for the lightning blindness to go away, then crept forward.

A few minutes later he was back on the highway in search of somewhere to spend the night.

Dave was just as prone as other men to let his emotions get away from him. Especially when he just suffered a traumatic loss.

But Dave wasn't that way when it came to combat. It didn't matter whether he was wearing the desert camouflage of the United States Marine Corps, or fighting his own personal war against the bad men of the world.

When he went to war, he put his game face on and his best foot forward. He carefully thought out every situation and planned accordingly.

Tonight he'd entered warrior mode. He'd declared war on Dalton's Raiders, despite Tony's admonition not to.

He couldn't help that part, anyway. His reasoning was simple. Killing one of his friends was almost as bad as killing one of his family.

Some things just could not go unpunished.

Tony had given his life to obtain news about the people who'd kidnapped Beth.

Dave was convinced his friend kept himself alive long enough to pass the information on to him.

He reasoned that since Beth was not in the hell hole which was Albuquerque, she was no longer in immediate danger.

And he could take care of business here before setting out after her again.

He also knew that night traveling without goggles, in a driving rainstorm, on a pitch black night, would be a fool's game. He'd move little more than walking pace. And after a long night on the road he'd be exhausted. And only halfway to his weapons.

No, it made much more sense to try to get some sleep. Difficult considering his present state of mind, sure. But if he could do it he'd have a much clearer head when the sun came up.

And he'd be a lot less likely to do something stupid.

## Chapter 41

Dave did manage to get five hours of very fitful sleep. It wasn't enough, but it was better than nothing.

When he awoke in the sleeper cab of the big orange Roadway tractor it took him a moment to regain his bearings. His mind was in a haze, from all the turmoil he'd suffered the night before, the trying to sleep in soggy clothing, the dehydration he felt from not having taken in liquids in twelve plus hours.

For several moments he wasn't even sure what he'd dreamed and what was real.

He saw the key to the Polaris on the tiny drop-down bedside table and he realized it was *all* real. Every bit of it, good and bad.

"I'm sorry, Tony. I let you down. I should have been there sooner."

In time, after he had a chance to think things over, Dave would realize he'd followed their plan to the letter. Tony had been on the street for at least three hours, slowly dying. They couldn't have burned him once the rain had started. And the rain started before Tony was overdue.

Dave didn't screw up. What happened to Tony was unfortunate. And preventable in several ways.

But Dave couldn't have followed their plan and prevented it.

For now, though, his blind rage wasn't letting him think things through. In his mind he caused Tony's death. Tony wasn't perfect by any means. But they were partners. Tony had stuck his neck out on Dave's behalf. And Dave had let him die.

He owed Tony.

And there was only one way he could pay him back.

By chopping off the head of the snake that bit him.

He stepped down from the tractor and looked at his watch. It had stopped during the night, but he didn't think it was from water damage.

From the angle of the sun he estimated it to be about oh eight hundred hours. He set his watch and wound it, happy to see the second hand start moving.

He looked around and saw no other souls in sight.

That was good. Whether any highway travelers might be friendly or not was not particularly relevant. He didn't much feel like dealing with them either way.

He picked up the backpack he'd retrieved from the highway after he left the Dalton compound the night before and peered inside.

The pack was soaked through and through, of course. But the soup and jerky he had left was okay.

Okay in that it had been protected from water damage and was still edible.

He just didn't have enough.

He removed a bottle of water and guzzled it on the spot.

That left two bottles.

He'd need more.

Dave's plan was to go off-road.

It was the only safe way to move by day on an all-terrain vehicle. If he drove along the highway he'd be visible for a mile or more. Anyone with a rifle could pick him off from a distance and merely walk to the crashed vehicle to retrieve it.

In all likelihood Dave would never even see the shooter before he died.

Night travel wasn't much better.

On an overcast night he'd have to move at a very low speed since he had no goggles. Otherwise he'd risk crashing into obstacles he wouldn't see until the very last second.

And at that speed, if he passed someone along the highway and didn't see them in the inky darkness, they could run up behind him and unload a full magazine before he even realized he'd been spotted.

No. He'd thought it through and decided the only safe way to move was well off the highway, keeping the highway in sight so he didn't get lost, but staying far enough away to be more or less safe.

He defined far enough as a thousand meters or so.

At that range only a man with a sniper rifle could pick him off, and he'd need a very steady hand and a great grasp of shooting fundamentals.

He walked off the highway and into the brush of a rest area park. The Polaris was still there, as he hoped it would be. He still had the key in his pocket. So he wasn't worried about anyone starting it and driving away.

But he'd had no tools when he parked it in the heavy rain. No way to remove the battery cable.

If someone with a little bit of no-how had stumbled across it, they might have been able to hotwire it.

Of course, they'd have no way of knowing it wasn't fried by the EMPs like the hundreds of other vehicles within a mile in either direction of it.

The vehicle had a small cargo bed, with a spare tire mounted behind the driver's seat with a bungee cord.

A second cord held two very important items tightly against the tire: a lug wrench and a pair of eighteen inch bolt cutters.

No jack was needed. The Polaris was light enough when empty to allow a grown man to lift any of the four corners and place it atop a block. As long as he had a spare, a lug wrench and something to shove under it, no jack was needed.

The bolt cutters weren't standard equipment for such a vehicle. They were added by Tony after the blackout, presumably to cut the metal tag seals and padlocks from trailers on the highway.

Dave had his own pair in the Explorer which was almost identical.

They weren't made for cutting barbed wire, necessarily.

But they'd do the trick quite nicely.

He returned to the highway and set out toward a long white trailer perhaps half a mile away. It said "Kroger's Grocers" on the side, although from that distance Dave couldn't make out the words. He recognized the color scheme, though. Dark green tractor, white trailer, orange wind deflector. He'd passed enough of the trucks during his travels to know what was in them.

He crossed his fingers and hoped the trailer would add some food and water to his supplies.

## Chapter 42

By the time Dave filled his backpack with food and bottled water, then made his way back to the Polaris, it was almost noon.

But he still had at least seven hours of daylight left.

And he could cover a hell of a lot of ground on a Polaris in seven hours, even going overland over muddy ground.

The Polaris was one of the best ATVs on the market. They were almost impossible to get stuck, almost never broke down and had enough power to climb up steep embankments.

Dave wasn't sure whether Tony had his choice of vehicles when he procured this thing from his prepper friend. But if he did, he made a wise choice indeed.

Before he left he topped off the tank, using a five gallon jerry can he took from a jeep on his way back from the Kroger's truck. The can was still half full, and he put it in the cargo bay of the ATV. Then he stepped aboard, fired it up, and drove due south until he was half a mile from the highway.

The barbed wire fences slowed him down. There were far more of them than he ever expected.

Dave had been born and raised in Texas. Driving up and down highways and county roads in Texas, one sees a lot of barbed wire fences. It's impossible to drive more than a mile without passing one. And they line most of the county and state highways.

He'd always assumed that was because Texas had so many cattle, which needed to be kept off the roads so they didn't become big four legged collision hazards.

And that much was true. But Dave was wrong in assuming the fencing was predominant only in cattle country.

New Mexico had just as much barbed wire as Texas. But far fewer cattle.

Actually, that wasn't quite true. Much of the fencing in New Mexico looked like barbed wire. But since there were few cattle on the huge tracts of scrub brush and desert in the Land of Enchantment, much of it was just wire.

No barbs. Just wire.

From a distance it looked just like barbed wire, but it didn't have the sharp points on it which cows hated brushing up against. And which encouraged them not to push against the wire and break it.

From Dave's perspective, the fact it had no barbs was irrelevant. It was still a pain in the ass.

He still had to get off his vehicle every few hundred yards to cut three strands of the stuff with his bolt cutters so he could proceed.

It slowed him down. But it was still the safest way to travel. And even though the ground he was traversing over was soft and muddy from the storm the night before, it was no match for the soft knobby tires of the Polaris.

Cutting the wires was a pain in the ass, but in the grand scheme of things it wasn't that big a deal.

What was a big deal was something Dave discovered after he'd cut some fencing and was climbing back onto the ATV.

Something caught his eye.

Something which caused him to fall to his knees on the muddy ground and wail like a banshee.

Something that would cause him distress and reawaken the rage he'd felt the evening before.

A large fly, one his grandpa would have called a horse fly, buzzed around Dave's head as he cut the three strands of wire and let them fall to the ground. He swatted at it with his free hand and missed it, but it flew away and left him alone.

And that was good enough for him.

As he climbed back onto the vehicle, though, he saw the fly again.

This time it flew into the passenger side cup holder, which Dave honestly hadn't paid much attention to at that point.

Perhaps if one of the Starbuck's had been open for business and he'd pulled up to the drive-through for a grande latte, he would have.

But those days were gone forever.

The fly flew into the cup holder and never came out, which piqued Dave's curiosity.

So he peered into it to see what the fly was doing.

He was immediately sickened, almost to the point of throwing up.

It was a human finger.

## Chapter 43

Dave removed it with two of his own fingers and held it at arm's length while he examined it.

It hadn't been torn off. It was severed with something tough enough to cut through the bone, almost down to the knuckle of the poor soul it once belonged to.

It appeared to be a man's finger, from the way it was calloused and rough. The nail wasn't manicured, and there was a considerable amount of dirt beneath the nail.

Certainly not uncommon in the post-apocalyptic world, where many people lived like animals.

He hoped it wasn't Tony's. And he'd probably never know. The night before, he'd focused on Tony's face as he lay dying with his head in Dave's lap, and on trying to hear Tony's last words.

It certainly never occurred to Dave to inspect his friend's hands and count his fingers.

The finger was fresh. It had turned gray, but was still pliable and hadn't yet started to decompose.

He hoped it wasn't Tony's, for that would mean they tortured him before they set him on fire. As though the burning itself didn't give them enough sadistic pleasure, they had to make him suffer first.

But then again, if it wasn't Tony's finger, then whose could it possibly be?

Were those madmen in the habit of brutally murdering more than one person in the same day?

Whoever's appendage it was, circumstances were vastly different now than they were the night before. Dave was no longer in enemy territory, running the risk of being discovered and shot at any moment.

It wasn't raining torrentially.

He didn't have a full body to bury, and no shovel to bury it with.

This time he could do better than just leave a body under a tree and ask God to watch over it for him.

Dave had always hated the term "remains."

In Iraq, a couple of his friends were blown to bits by improvised explosive devices. So much so that the pieces had to be meticulously collected.

He caught a peek at the manifest on the day an Air Force C-17 cargo plane came to pick up the flag-draped coffin of one of those buddies.

The manifest listed his friend as:

Remains, human, Corp Robert L. Taylor, USMC

Dave had been overcome with grief that day, and yelled at the plane's loadmaster, an Air Force Technical Sergeant.

"He's not *remains*, damn you! He's a man. A good man. He left behind a wife and three children. He's a United States Marine. He's not *remains*."

He was overcome with grief and behaved badly. To pacify him, the loadmaster scratched out the word "remains" on the manifest  and replaced it with "damn fine Marine."

Dave looked for the man again every time a C-17 touched down but never saw him again. He wanted to apologize. He wanted to explain he knew it wasn't the loadmaster's fault. That it was just the military's way of dealing with things.

And to that very day, five years later, Dave still hated the term: *remains*. It just left a very sour taste in his mouth.

He'd been limited by circumstances in what he could do for Tony. But if this was a small piece of his friend, he'd at least do the proper thing for part of him.

If it wasn't him... if it wasn't part of Tony, then it once belonged to someone else who went against the Dalton clan in some form or fashion.

And that fact: that he was Dalton's enemy, automatically made him Dave's ally. Whoever's finger it was, Dave would give it its proper due.

He had no shovel. But then again, he didn't have to dig a full-sized grave.

A shoebox-sized hole would do.

And the cutting blade of the bolt cutters would do quite nicely in the soft mud.

It just didn't seem proper not to wrap the finger in... something.

But Dave was limited in what he had. So a sock would have to do.

He spoke to the finger as he prepared it, as though he were talking to Tony.

"I'm sorry I don't have something cleaner, or more appropriate. But I figure this is better than laying you directly into the dirt. And maybe it'll take a few days for the worms to chew through the sock before they start eating you. I know, you're way beyond caring. But right is right."

He placed the finger in the bottom of the sock, then twisted it a couple of times and wrapped it back over itself once again.

Then he placed it gently into the bottom of his hole and raked the mud back over it.

Lastly, he stood over the tiny grave, bowed his head, and said a brief prayer:

*Lord, please take and keep this token and the soul of the man it once belonged to. Whoever he was, whatever he did in this life, he was a man created in your image and therefore deserving of your mercy.*

*Please take him into your care, forgive him for his sins, and give him a place in Your kingdom.*

*In your holy name,*

*Amen.*

He was stopped anyway, and the engine on the Polaris was off. This seemed as appropriate a time as any to refill his belly and satisfy his thirst.

It seemed an odd time and place to eat a meal, but it was as good a place as any. And the new world had become essentially a great big graveyard. Bodies, regardless of the way they became such, were now left in the open all over the place.

As he ate a can of Dinty Moore beef stew, Dave tried to remember the last time he went a full twenty four hour day without seeing at least one dead human, propped up in an abandoned car with his head torn apart by a self-inflicted wound. Or lying beside the road where a bandit left him to rot.

It had been so long he couldn't remember.

Months, maybe.

He decided for the thousandth time he didn't like the new world.

Not much at all.

## Chapter 44

After Dave traveled several miles he turned his attention to the ribbon of highway he'd been following half a mile away.

He watched it looking for a particular landmark.

He'd hidden his weapons at an office park, a strip mall next to the highway. Beneath a mountain of garbage directly adjacent to several overloaded dumpsters.

He couldn't remember the mile marker on the highway directly in front of the place. And he didn't really need it. As long as he remembered a red cement mixer, directly in front of a Chevy Silverado towing a bass boat, directly in front of a Mayflower moving van, he could find his weapons again. His Explorer would be parked in the right lane of the highway about a quarter mile beyond the series of vehicles.

By his calculations, he was getting close. No more than a mile and a half to two miles away now.

He'd have to be careful not to pass it by.

There was no reason to believe he'd been spotted. He'd heard no gunshots that would have forced him to go to ground or speed out of there. He was well aware there were nomads walking back and forth along the highway, crawling in and out of the trucks looking for food.

But really, how often did they take the time and trouble to peer out onto the horizon? And even if they did, he'd appear no bigger than an insect atop his four-wheeler.

Those who did see him would write him off for the most part, assuming he was a hunter out for game. They might be surprised he was atop a working vehicle. Or more likely, wouldn't even notice he was. From that distance it might be hard to make out what was beneath him, and they might just assume he was on horseback.

Another hour and several more cut fences and he finally saw the series of vehicles on the highway he was looking for.

His timing couldn't have been more perfect. The sun would be setting within the hour. Another and it would be dark enough for him to drive the Polaris a bit closer to the highway, and then to abandon it in heavy brush.

He'd make note of where he left it by memorizing the mile marker. And if his memory faltered, as it sometimes did in recent months, he'd simply look once again for his vehicles and their relation to the ATV.

He had some time to kill, which he normally hated. But in this case he was exhausted. Taxed not only by the events of the previous day, but by the fitful and restless night he'd had in the sleeper cab following.

If he'd had a flat place to lie he'd have napped.

And he did- have a flat place, that is. The ground in this particular part of New Mexico was flat as a pancake.

But it was still soaked from the rain.

Having spent the previous evening and all night long in wet clothing, he was sick of it. His clothes had now dried and he much preferred for them to stay that way.

He did the next best thing. He lifted up the armrests between the two seats and moved to the passenger seat, then leaned over on his side and put his head in the driver's seat.

Atop his backpack.

The pack was great for carrying rations, but it really sucked as a pillow.

Still, it was better than nothing.

The two side by side seats would never pass for a bed. But at least he was more or less prone, and still, and reasonably certain no one would walk up on him.

Under the circumstances it was the best he could do.

He wasn't fooling himself. He knew he'd never doze off in his current position. It was just too darned uncomfortable.

And he was way too tense.

But as long as he could close his eyes and rest them, it wasn't a bad way to kill an hour.

He was surprised when he woke up thirty five minutes later and realized he had indeed dozed off.

He was obviously more tired than he thought.

He sat up and immediately regretted it.

Lying in such a position for so long made him stiff. In his back, his neck, his legs.

But at least the pain jarred him awake.

The sun was going down and he was treated to an absolutely beautiful sunset. It reminded him that the desert has its own kind of beauty that many people never experience.

He wondered how many more sunsets he'd have to endure alone before he finally got his family back together again.

Dave was a simple man. He never longed for much in life. A few dollars in the bank. The love of a good woman. The security of knowing he could have and raise children in a safe environment in the greatest country in the world.

He never bargained for this… any of it. If his family had been in San Antonio when the lights went out, he'd never have had reason to leave.

Unfortunately, Dave wasn't allowed to pick the circumstances surrounding the blackout. The timing was atrocious, coming at the exact time Sarah and the girls were on a plane heading to a place a thousand miles away.

Going after them was never in question. Neither was going after Beth.

As many times as he'd wished this was all a very bad dream it wasn't. He'd dealt with it thus far as best he could, and he'd continue to do so. No matter how long it took, no matter how many people he had to kill to get there.

He'd get there. That wasn't in question either.

As the skies grew darker he cranked the wheeler back up and turned north toward the highway, inching forward at a mile an hour or so. He'd chosen his target before he napped, a stand of mesquite brush just adjacent to the bass boat.

A crack of thunder in the distance surprised him. He thought the rain was finished with him.

But the prevailing winds were chasing the thunder and would probably blow the front clear of him.

The skies overhead were cloudy but not so much so. The moon was in crescent and mostly obscured.

The night would be dark, but that wouldn't be a problem. For the first place he'd head after he hid the wheeler would be to his Explorer.

The night vision goggles he'd stashed beneath his passenger seat would make the rest of what he had to do so much easier.

## Chapter 45

Dave checked his watch as he stood before the mountain of garbage, waiting for two voices in the darkness to pass him by.

It was twenty one hundred, give or take a bit.

He'd never be sure, since he occasionally let his watch wind down and had to reset it based upon the position of the sun.

Twenty minutes slow or fast didn't matter much.

He had a good ballpark number and figured that was good enough.

The voices passed and he moved aside several garbage bags until he found what he'd come there for. A canvas military deployment bag full of various rifles and handguns, ammunition, his crossbow and bolts, and several hand grenades given to him by Karen's neighbors outside Kansas City.

He strapped on his sidearm, and for the first time in days didn't feel totally vulnerable. There was something oddly soothing about knowing one had the ability to defend oneself against aggressors.

He silently vowed he'd never let anyone talk him into being unarmed again.

The bag was heavy. Close to a hundred pounds.

He wouldn't attack until the following night. It would take him awhile to get close to the Dalton's compound, and the night would be half gone by then.

He didn't want to go to battle limited by time. Nor did he want the sun to rise halfway through his campaign. For darkness was one of his most loyal friends.

No, his plan was to move forward on this night. To get into position half a mile from his target. Then to hide his weapons again and to get some rest.

He'd formed a plan. It was methodical and well-thought out. But it depended on his being well rested and alert.

There was also the element of surprise to consider. Had he had weapons the previous night on the Daltons' porch he'd have had the advantage. But he couldn't attack with just his bare hands.

He lost the element of surprise when he stole the Polaris and left the compound. In essence, he alerted Dalton that someone had been on their turf.

Someone who was bold enough to steal from them right from under their drug-impaired noses.

Surely, even in their drugged up stupor, they could see that such a person was a danger to them.

Dave expected, once they'd determined Tony had been moved and his Polaris was missing, that they'd be on high alert.

The sentries would have been beefed up. With their best people, not just some miscreants occupying space and killing time.

There would be snipers hidden in the trees. The porch would be fortified with sandbags. Vehicles would be rolled into the yard to act as barricades, their tires flattened.

Dave expected diversions.

Some of the gang would take up positions in adjacent houses, in order to pin down any aggressors with crossfire. And to provide ready reinforcements for the headquarters if the need called.

He also expected a recall, of all the gang members, from wherever they might be on the gang's extensive turf.

He expected Crazy Town to be on the same war footing he was.

Because that's what he'd have done if his name was Dalton.

He was already tired when he finished lugging the heavy bag to the Explorer and opened up the hatch. When he hefted it up, it seemed like it had doubled in weight. It was going to be a long night.

He'd intentionally wait until past midnight to head out. By then the nomads would all be bedded down for the night, for nobody liked to travel in the hours of darkness.

Dave didn't mind, because he had the goggles to light his way. It was an eerie greenish-gray glow which made everything look rather surreal. But it beat the hell out of stumbling around in the darkness trying to feel your way around.

He tried to relax, as he sat in the seat of the Explorer. But he was way too tense. He knew the next couple of days were going to be sheer hell.

But he also knew he had a mission to perform. And he wouldn't be able to live with himself if he didn't get it done.

## Chapter 47

At one minute past midnight Tony turned the key on the auxiliary ignition he'd installed on the dashboard.

Nothing.

He started to curse his bad luck, then cursed his stupidity instead.

He'd removed the negative battery cable and placed it in his weapons bag on the night he'd parked the damn thing, just to keep somebody from trying to hotwire it.

Back out of the vehicle and back to the back, where he retrieved the cable and reinstalled it.

As he crawled back in the drivers seat he grumbled, "Well, this is already turning into a goat rope."

Indeed, it wasn't starting well.

He was already beat, and at ten miles an hour would need another hour and a half to get past the Dalton's Raiders' exit ramp. It would take another hour to hide his weapons again. And probably another to find a sleeper cab which wasn't occupied.

There were two bright spots as he saw them.

First of all, once he was situated he could sleep the remainder of the night away and late into the next afternoon. He'd go into his campaign well rested.

Second, the heavy thunderstorms from the previous day had brought with them a cold front. For the first time in a long time he could count on sleeping soundly.

Those two things, he reasoned, would go a long way toward evening his odds.

Sure, they may outnumber him twenty or thirty or forty to one.

But as stupid as they'd already shown themselves to be, he expected them to continue their drug use, continue their partying.

He fully expected them to be at least partially impaired.

Dead would be better. Comatose would be good. But he'd settle for impaired.

He drove off hoping nothing else went wrong.

Shortly before oh two hundred Dave parked his Explorer about fifty yards in front of a tractor trailer rig, as was his habit from the beginning.

He hoped the sleeper cab was available. If it was already occupied, he'd have to search for another, but there were several in the area. He was confident he'd find a place to sleep. Worst case scenario, he'd pop up the one man tent he always carried in the Explorer's cargo bay.

The first thing to do, though, was to hide his weapons.

Dave was a big believer in not fixing things that weren't broken. Along that same vein of thinking, he would stick with something which had worked in the past until such time it failed him.

Just south of the Explorer, on the eastbound access road of Interstate 40, was a huge apartment complex.

Dave's experience was that, in the days immediately following the blackout, most residents stayed in their homes. They were afraid because bad men were roaming the streets, taking what they needed at the end of a gun.

At that time, most residents naively believed that the blackout was temporary. That at any time, the power company would restore the power, and they'd figure out why in hell all the vehicles stopped running at the same time.

Most households had at least a few days supply of water and food.

Granted the food wasn't the best.

The lucky ones had canned goods and boxes of cereal and maybe some pasta to sustain their families for several days.

The less fortunate might have to settle for packages of old Jell-O and turkey gravy from the top shelves of their cupboards, long forgotten and covered in dust.

The really unfortunate ones had to start eating their dog's or cat's food after a day or two.

The taps stopped running almost immediately when the water plant's pumps shut down. They'd had generator backups, of course. But the generators were fried at the same time as the electrical grid.

Once again, the good planners and the lucky had bottled water. The poor planners and the unlucky had no such thing.

And the stupid among them used their bottled water to wash up so they smelled pretty.

They'd never been up against something like this before. So it wasn't really their fault.

Actually, it was. That was really, really dumb.

What was even sadder was the number of people who never knew they could drink the water from their hot water heaters in a pinch.

And from their toilet tanks when they really got thirsty.

That was water which was already in place when the water plant's pumps stopped pumping.

All over Albuquerque, people tried to put on a brave face and remain patient for the first days, confident that everything would be okay.

It was during those days they tried their best to carry on a semblance of routine life.

They continued to dutifully carry the household garbage to the dumpsters.

Until the dumpsters started to overflow because there were no garbage trucks running with which to empty them.

Once the dumpsters were full, bags of garbage started piling up in front of them.

Huge mountains of garbage were soon formed.

The piles served their purpose. They got the garbage out of the homes.

The residents who created them, though, never realized they'd serve a second, equally important purpose.

They made excellent hiding places.

## Chapter 48

Beth had to admit it. Although she hadn't bonded well with old Sal... mostly because he could be a great big grouch, she'd grown quite fond of the woman she called Grandma Nellie.

Nellie was one of the kindest souls she'd ever met.

Of course, Beth was only eight. Her collection of friends was somewhat limited.

But she knew a lot of other adults. Her former teachers. Neighbors back in San Antonio. Those gray haired church ladies who even she could see smiled to somebody's face and then gossiped behind their backs.

The only woman Beth had ever known who was as genuinely kind as Grandma Nellie was her real grandmother. Grandma Elizabeth, who she was named after.

Grandma Elizabeth died a full year before the blackout, but she and her namesake had had a magical relationship. Sarah had made arrangements for the school bus to drop Beth off at the nursing home where Grandma Elizabeth lived, and they spent time together every afternoon until Sarah got off work.

They took turns reading to one another.

Elizabeth's vision was about gone, and she could no longer read the classic novels she'd enjoyed over and over again her adult life.

But she could read Dr. Seuss books, with their oversized fonts. It seemed half-inch high words were the only words she could actually read herself, and thus boosted her self-worth and self-esteem.

So even though Beth complained to everyone else she was way too old to have someone read *Horton Hears a Who* and *One Fish, Two Fish, Red Fish, Blue Fish* to her, she'd never tell that to Grandma Elizabeth.

They had a system. Grandma Elizabeth tired easily. So she'd read Dr. Seuss to Beth, while Beth sat at her bedside holding the old woman's hand and pretending to cling to every word.

When Grandma Elizabeth began to fade and nod off, Beth would take the children's book and put it aside. She'd read *Gone With the Wind* or *The Grapes of Wrath* until the old woman drifted off to sleep, then mark her page for the next time.

And while her grandmother slept, Beth would continue to hold and caress her hand. She was fascinated with her grandmother's hands. They were so strong, yet looked so ancient. Beth liked to run her fingertips over the raised blue veins while she slept, then to turn them over and pretend to read Elizabeth's fortune when she was awake.

Only once did Dave ever raise his concern about Beth reading such books.

"The language can be a bit salty, Mom. And the subject matter... civil war and slavery? Isn't that too much for a child of her age?"

Elizabeth had pooh-poohed his opinion.

"Those are classics, young man. She'll never be able to consider herself grown up and refined until she reads them. Might as well get her started early, and build in her a love for good literature before she gets hooked on comic books and trash."

Elizabeth was never one to either mince words or withhold her opinion. And Dave shut up immediately, for his mother was one people didn't argue with.

Little Beth once asked her about her hands and why they appeared to be a million years old.

"Why child," she admonished. "That's just not so. They're only half a million years old. And they tell a story. Everyone's hands do."

"What do you mean, Grandmother?"

"Count the veins, child. An old woman will have a raised vein for every man she ever loved. And every wrinkle represents a man who loved her.

"Every freckle indicates a child who warmed her heart with a smile. Do you see the dark spots? The ones which look like freckles, only they're black?"

"Yes, ma'am."

"Those are liver spots. But they've got nothing to do with liver. They actually come from grief. An old woman gets a new liver spot every time someone she loves passes away. And every little scar? Those represent each time a man has broken her heart.

"So you can see, dear child, that I've lived a long life. I've had good times and bad. I've loved and been loved, and I'm going to leave behind some of the finest people on God's earth. And you, child, are my favorite one of all."

"But if I'm your favorite, what about Lindsey?"

"Your sister is my second favorite. She'd be my first, except you come by to read to me and she doesn't."

She winked at little Beth in a conspiratorial manner and said, "But that's our secret, honey. Don't ever tell Lindsey, or you'll hurt her feelings."

For a very long time Beth was on cloud nine. Being told she was her grandmother's favorite gave her a sense she was very special indeed.

The old woman in the red pickup, the one she called Grandma Nellie, had the same hands and the same temperament.

Although she was only eight, Beth was bright beyond compare. She didn't understand the reasons an old person's mind starts to falter. But she could see Nellie's was gone. At the same time, though, she sensed it wasn't Nellie's fault, and that she mustn't be punished for it.

Rather, she applied the same gentle care she'd given her own grandmother in the last months before her death.

She held Nellie's hand. She read to her. She talked with the old woman for hours at a time.

She developed a game with Nellie. As old Sal steered the horses down the long stretches of highway, she and Nellie looked at the clouds.

"Okay, Grandma," Beth would tell Nellie. "The first one to find a teddy bear in the clouds wins." Then a puppy. Then a slipper. Then a kitten. They entertained themselves for hours.

They became more than friends. They became more like... family.

Beth allowed Nellie to call her Becky. Because she knew that was the only way Nellie would ever see her: as her own departed granddaughter.

With Sal she cut no such slack. Sal knew going in that her name was Beth. That she was no relation. That knowledge strained their relationship. And although she now knew Sal wasn't the devil she first thought him to be... that he was a kind man who'd protect her at all costs, she'd never offer him the affection she gave so willingly to Nellie.

Life at Benny's place was so much easier than it had been on the road. It was permanent, for one thing. The scenery didn't change from day, nor did the challenges of trying to stay alive.

The people at Benny's place were friendly for the most part. Despite Beth's wildly imaginative talk of staging a rebellion to overthrow the patriarch, she had to admit she'd seen much worse places to be.

In fact, life at Benny's wasn't that bad, considering how the rest of the world was living. It was stable, it was safe, and she was surrounded by people who seemed to care for one another.

It reminded Beth of her Aunt Karen's farm in Kansas, in the early days following the blackout.

Before all those bad men overran the farm and shot Uncle Tommy and the other men.

Before they'd taken over the place and ran it like a prison.

All in all, Beth missed her Mommy and Daddy and her sister Lindsey. She cried herself to sleep some nights thinking about them. But she had the unrequited love of an old woman who adored her. And that would help sustain her until her father finally came.

It had been a long day. Thom had been teasing her again about her freckles and she finally got angry enough to punch him in the arm. He wailed like a little girl and Beth was reprimanded and sent to her room without dessert.

She needed hugs and snuggles and the reassurance that she was loved. So she did what she often did.

She went upstairs and crawled into bed with Grandma Nellie. Grandma Nellie always had love and snuggles to give her little Becky.

Only tonight she didn't.

Tonight she was very cold and unresponsive.

Tonight she was dead.

## Chapter 49

Beth would feel many things in the coming days. She'd feel the dreadful agony one feels when a loved one dies. That would be the biggest thing.

But she'd feel other things as well. Things she couldn't understand. Things that made no sense to her and left her feeling confused and angry.

She'd feel disappointment in Nellie. Nellie had told her she'd always be there for her. Nellie had let her down.

She felt resentment for old Sal. Although she could see he was hurting too, she felt no sympathy for him. Instead, her mindset went back to the days when he'd first removed her from her Aunt Karen's farm. He was once again the evil man who'd stolen her.

No, he was worse than that. He was the evil man who'd stolen her, and who had let Nellie die. He was her husband. Wasn't it his job to keep her alive?

She blamed old Sal exclusively for taking away the one person in Benny's compound she really and truly cared about.

Nellie was buried in a simple plot in the northern corner of Benny's acreage. She wasn't the first one buried there, and certainly wouldn't be the last.

Instead of marble or granite headstones, which were apparently hard to procure since the blackout, a three hundred pound boulder was rolled onto the grave once the service was over.

A relative who proclaimed to be an artist, but who obviously couldn't spell, painted the following on Nellie's boulder in crude block letters:

Here Lies
NELLIE AMBROSIO
She was loved by all
She will be mised

Beth wasn't the only one left suffering.

The day after Nellie was laid to rest Sal went into the mother of all funks.

He wasn't talking to anyone. He wasn't eating. He wasn't sleeping.

He was barely alive.

The only one he was even responding to was little Beth.

And she started to feel sorry for him.

Sorry enough to go to him. To hold his hand. And to tell him she was there for him.

He'd turn to look at her, but his eyes would be in some distant place.

He'd squeeze her hand but say nothing.

He was in bad shape.

## Chapter 50

Dave, of course, knew nothing of Nellie's death or Sal's condition.

He was still convinced the pair were brutal slave traders who'd imprisoned his baby, and were making her do backbreaking labor. And perhaps other unspeakable things as well.

He had no sympathy for either of them.

And he was coming for them with every intention of making sure they died miserable deaths.

First, though, Dave had another mission to complete.

He'd finally crawled into a sleeper cab's bunk about three that morning. He'd been so tired he fell asleep within seconds.

When he awoke, he thought he'd only dozed off. He expected the sun to be up shortly.

Then he finally looked at his watch. It said twenty one hundred hours. Nine p.m.

He'd quite literally slept the whole day away.

No wonder his muscles were so damn stiff.

He crawled out of the bunk and stretched, then peered through the windshield of the big rig.

It was spotted with drizzle.

The rain was coming back.

Peachy. Just peachy.

But then again, the rain was his friend two nights before and helped cover his egress from the enemy's compound.

Perhaps he needed to stop bitching about things and become a "glass is half full" kind of guy.

Perhaps.

He sat in the driver's seat and tried to shake the cobwebs from his head so he could formulate a new plan. One which would account for the rain.

And when he was finished it was a simple one: Go in and kill all the bastards any way he could.

Admittedly it wasn't the most thought out plan he'd ever devised.

But he was ready to implement it anyway.

He returned to the sleeper long enough to strap on his sidearm, replace the knife into his boot, and to grab his AR-15 rifle.

Then he climbed out of the cab and onto the pavement below.

He scanned the area in all directions. The only movement he detected was about a quarter mile away. Three men walking down the highway in the opposite direction. Taking their sweet time.

He didn't remember voices, but assumed it was their talking as they walked past his truck which had awakened him.

In the upper right corner of the goggles the power monitor reflected two of six bars. From past experience he knew he had maybe four hours of battery life left.

The prudent thing to do would be to replace the batteries.

But they were hard to come by. He only had a dozen left, and they had to last him for awhile.

The next best thing was to take spare batteries with him, and he made a mental note to remove some from his weapons bag.

He looked around again, just to be sure he was alone, then stole away into the darkness toward the garbage pile which held the rest of his weapons. Along the way he said a silent prayer, asking God to help him get through the night intact.

"Not for me," he made certain he specified. "I don't deserve it. Please spare me for little Beth's sake. So I can go and liberate her next."

As he finished his prayer a bolt of lightning struck a tree two hundred yards in front of him.

He wasn't sure whether it was God telling him he understood Dave's request and would honor it.

Or whether it was God telling him he was an idiot for going into a hostile situation totally alone.

He made it to the garbage pile without an indication of any other movement in any direction.

So far, so good.

The easy thing to do would be to go through the bag and decide which weapons he'd need, then leave the rest behind for another fight another day.

The trouble with that was that he had no idea how many bad guys he'd encounter, or under what circumstances. He didn't know if it would be over quickly, or whether he'd be involved in several prolonged firefights.

He didn't know whether he'd have the opportunity to apply guerilla tactics, which he considered his specialty, or whether all the fighting was going to be a bare-knuckle, all out brawl.

In other words, he didn't know squat.

He didn't know which weapons he'd need, or how much ammo to take.

And it was a situation where taking the wrong weapons or insufficient ammo could cost him his life.

So the only prudent thing to do was to take it all.

Lugging a hundred pounds worth of guns, ammo and grenades wouldn't be easy. Nor would it be subtle. It would slow him down and reduce his chances of slipping in unnoticed.

He felt he had no choice.

He hefted the bag and manhandled it to the far side of the highway from the Crazy Town checkpoint and moved it a little at a time, from the cover of one abandoned car to the next.

The night vision goggles gave him a distinct advantage, although he always had to be mindful the bad guys could have them as well.

They didn't have them, or at least weren't wearing them, the first time he infiltrated their camp.

But that was before they were invaded. Before someone came in right under their noses, took a valuable vehicle, and then left unmolested.

Things would be different now.

They'd be watching out for him this time.

Presumably with all the manpower, all the firepower, and all the tools they had available to them.

## Chapter 51

At another time, under other circumstances, Dave would be cursing the rain.

This time, it was a familiar friend. It had helped him two nights before, and he hoped it would do so again.

But like every woman he'd ever known she'd have a mischievous side to contend with. The rain brought with it the lightning, which would periodically take away the advantage his goggles gave him. In fact, several times a minute the lightning would flash, and would appear several times brighter through his goggles than it would to someone not so equipped.

There was a chance his goggles might cause him to be blinded temporarily at a crucial time.

Like for example when he was lining up a shot or trying to take cover.

He might have to ditch the goggles at some point. But for now, for the first part of his operation, they were coming in very handy.

The rain was light. For now. But he knew it could turn torrential at any time.

It didn't rain often in the desert environment that was Albuquerque, New Mexico. But when it rained, as the saying goes, it poured.

So the rain, and the lightning it brought with it, might be an ally or foe. He wasn't sure which. But he'd progress slowly until he found out for sure.

He entered Crazy Town at the same place he had two nights before, moving gingerly from the abandoned cars on the highway to those on the service road beneath it.

This time, though, instead of progressing directly to the Dalton's Raiders' headquarters, he'd take a detour.

Enemy combatants are enemy combatants, no matter where one finds them or what they might be doing at the time. In Dave's estimation, it made sense to pick off the easy ones any chance he got to lessen the chance they'd be called in as reinforcements against him later.

He considered the sentries at the checkpoint to be easy targets of opportunity. He'd already evaluated their habits during his previous excursion to determine whether they were sloppy, lazy or stupid.

In his estimation, they were all three.

Of course, a smart leader would have moved the slackers out by now and replaced them with his elite guard. He wouldn't know for sure about that until he assaulted them. But just knowing whether that was the case would tell Dave a lot about the capabilities and tactics of the men he was dealing with.

And so far he wasn't impressed.

He made his way across the service road and to the same alley he'd used before to traverse the distance to the headquarters. He was lucky in that no lightning bolts lit him up and made him a sitting duck.

He hoped his luck held as he searched a row of houses until he found what he was looking for.

The third house from the corner was not only abandoned, it had been burned as well. He went through its back gate and lugged his heavy weapons bag into the back yard and up to the charred remnants of the house.

The rain was moderate now. Enough to limit visibility on both sides, but not so much he wouldn't be able to use all the weapons at his disposal. He'd never fired his crossbow under such conditions, and he wouldn't had there been a driving rain. But in a moderate rain he saw no potential impact on his bolts as they flew swiftly through the air, other than maybe taking a slight drop.

And he could adjust for a little droppage.

He took the crossbow from the bag and set it aside, then loaded his bolt rack, then the weapon itself.

He was tempted to take a hand grenade. He hadn't used one since Fallujah, but he remembered their impact. Not just on the unfortunate bodies which got in their way, but on the morale of the men who'd just seen their buddies torn to shreds.

He suspected that the sentries, knowing they were fighting a man with such weapons, would drop their guns and scatter like the wind.

The problem was, an explosion would attract attention and take away another ally: the element of surprise.

No, this first assault had to be silent. He couldn't announce his presence. Not just yet.

He guzzled a bottle of water, then another. His backpack was unnecessary weight and would be left behind with the weapons bag. And he didn't know how long his campaign would last. This would be his base of operations, this shell of a house hidden behind a six foot privacy fence. He might be in Crazy Town for only a few hours. Or it might be days. In any event, he didn't know when or how often he'd get the chance to come back here. He couldn't allow himself to become dehydrated if it was many hours.

He took a third bottle of water and shoved it into the upper pocket on his right leg.

Into the calf pocket on the same leg he put two magazines for his 9 mm handgun. He didn't expect to use it. It was a close range weapon. But he couldn't afford to run out of ammo if he did need it. He didn't mind dying against a superior aggressor in a fair fight. But he didn't want to die the humiliating death of an idiot who didn't plan for every scenario.

Into each pocket on his left leg he placed two magazines for his AR-15.

He shoved the weapons bag and his backpack beneath a half-burned piece of plywood and made his way back to the alley, where he exited the yard through the same back gate he'd used minutes before.

The alley wasn't paved, and the wheel ruts from once-frequent garbage trucks were muddy from the rain.

He'd have left very visible footprints if he'd moved down the center of the alley, so he stuck to the grassy areas next to the fences.

They provided much better cover anyway.

A few minutes later he was within spitting distance of the checkpoint sentries, sizing them up from his cover behind an abandoned Subaru.

## Chapter 52

If the men he was watching had been his Marines, Dave would have been pissed.

Since they were the enemy, not so much.

In fact, Dave couldn't have been more pleased, for it was apparent they hadn't learned anything from his excursion into the camp two nights before.

One was standing outside the Town Car, holding an umbrella in one hand and a lit cigarette in the other. He was wearing a black Old Navy hoodie and his rifle was slung over his shoulder. He was leaning against the car and giving maybe half his attention to his job.

And he was actually humming to himself, to some tune Dave couldn't quite make out through the raindrops.

Dave wondered how many others were in the car.

It was impossible to tell. But he had to assume they had working radios, even though he couldn't see one on the smoker. It may well have been hidden beneath his clothing to protect it from the rain.

He had to dispatch all of them. If he hit only one, the others would raise the alarm as soon as they found him. If he just bypassed them and went on to hit the headquarters, the HQ would call them in as reinforcements.

No, he had to take them all out.

The smoker put out his cigarette and checked his watch. Then he sauntered over to the car and rapped twice on the passenger side window.

The door opened and a second man stepped out. The umbrella changed hands first, and then the rifle. The smoker took his turn inside the dry car and the new man started pacing back and forth outside.

There were at least two of them, obviously rotating shifts in the rain. The trouble was, Dave didn't know how long the shifts were or how many more men were waiting in the car to take their turns.

He could answer both questions by waiting patiently. He hunkered down and tried his best to relax.

Exactly thirty minutes later, the second man went back to the window and rapped on it.

Dave was happy to see the man in the Old Navy hoodie step out to take his turn again.

There was only the two of them, taking turns in the rain every thirty minutes.

He checked his watch. It was, by his reckoning, five minutes after midnight.

He moved to a new position, a bit closer and with the light wind at his back.

His firing position.

Dave wasn't sure what impact the rain would have on his crossbow's bolt as it flew through the air. Maybe none. Just to be safe, though, he'd assume a bit of droppage was inevitable as the bolt flew the twenty yards or so between him and his target. He'd shoot just a bit high to allow for that.

He also had to fire when the man was far enough away from the Town Car not to fall on it or against it. He couldn't alert the man inside there was anything amiss.

His aim would have to be true. He had to drop the man in a single shot. He couldn't afford to allow him the opportunity to call out, or to fall against the hood of the car, or to fall out of Dave's sight and let him use his radio to call for reinforcements.

This might well be the most important shot Dave had ever made.

Of course, weren't all of them?

Luckily, Old Navy seemed a nervous sort. Or maybe he was just bored. He spent a good portion of his watch pacing back and forth.

Dave checked the time frequently.

There wasn't much else to do. His crossbow was already charged and ready to fire.

He was already in position, behind a 1974 Camaro which looked very much like the one his best friend owned in high school. All he had to do was rise, brace himself, and fire.

Old Navy was pacing, back and forth, first walking directly toward Dave, then doing an about face and walking away from him.

He was several feet from the front of the Town Car.

At twelve twenty five the rain picked up considerably and Dave started to wonder if he should aim his shot even higher on his target. But he decided not to. The bolt would fly at great velocity. Certainly too fast to gather a lot of water. Certainly not enough to weigh it down appreciably.

He hoped.

At least the rain would help deaden the sound of the man as he fell. And any sound he might make when he was hit.

He looked at his watch one last time. It was twelve thirty.

Go time.

His target was still pacing back and forth. It would have been easier for Dave to just shoot the man in the back as he walked away from him.

But Dave wasn't that way. He could not, would not, shoot a man in the back under any circumstances.

It wasn't considered civilized or fair back in the days of the old west. And in Dave's mind it still wasn't.

As the man walked with his back to Dave, Dave rose up from behind the old Camaro and leaned over its hood. He braced himself, held his breath and got ready to fire.

Old Navy turned and began walking back toward Dave, although he had no goggles and had no idea he was getting ready to die. From that distance, in the dark and with the rain beating down upon both of them, he couldn't see Dave or his crossbow.

Dave squeezed the trigger, aiming at the top of the man's heart.

The man gasped and dropped his cigarette, a look of surprise overtaking his face.

He fell to his knees, then face forward onto the pavement in front of him.

He made no effort to turn his head or close his eyes for he was dead before his face hit the street.

## Chapter 53

So far so good.

Dave left the crossbow on the hood of the Camaro and drew his knife from his boot. He made his way to the window of the Town Car and checked his watch again.

At twelve thirty five, exactly half an hour after the sentries had last changed positions, Dave rapped on the window of the car.

He heard cursing from within the car. The second sentry obviously had no desire to get back out into the downpour.

And in that regard, Dave would help him. For he wouldn't have to.

As the man stepped out, Dave's first thrust was to the throat.

It was quick and on target, and meant to keep the man from crying out.

As he expected, both of the man's hands went immediately to his throat and his face expressed a feeling of terror.

With his chest left unguarded, it was easy for Dave to ensure his second thrust was true as well.

Straight through the heart.

The man fell backward, his upper body in the car, his legs still being pummeled by the rain.

He got half his wish, anyway. Half of him would remain dry.

Dave took the man's handgun from its holster. Then he went to Old Navy and relieved him of his own handgun and the AK-47 he'd worn over his shoulder.

Dave didn't need the weapons.

But he couldn't afford to leave them either.

He knew nothing of the enemy's strength, or their firepower.

They might have hundreds of men, and hundreds of weapons.

Or they might have so few weapons they had to share between them.

In any event, leaving the weapons here would mean they might be used against him.

And that just wouldn't do.

He retrieved his crossbow and ran into the yard of the house on the corner. There he heaved the rifle and the handguns onto the house's roof.

He knew where they were, and could retrieve them later if he needed them.

But the bad guys would have no clue where to find them.

## Chapter 54

Beth Speer was wise beyond her eight short years.

She knew that she was an outsider. That she didn't belong to these people. That she was taken against her will and without her mother's knowledge.

Taken away to a place far away from everyone she'd ever known and loved.

It wasn't right, that they'd taken her. She knew that. But she'd also sensed the old woman had needed her. That in the old woman's eyes she was someone else. Someone who'd brought the old woman so much happiness.

Beth could also see that she could fill that role. She could bring the light back into the old woman's eyes. And she was more than willing to do so.

Because Beth was just that way.

And after all, the woman she called Grandma Nellie was kind to her. As kind as anyone had ever been.

Beth was happy to ease her pain. To coddle her and pretend to be someone she wasn't. It hurt nobody, but made Nellie so much happier.

But now Nellie was gone and things had changed so much.

Now it was the old man's turn to be in a miserable state.

Sal had loved Becky as much as Nellie did. He was just as torn as she when their little granddaughter died.

The difference was that Nellie was wracked with dementia. In her mind Becky and Beth were one and the same. In her troubled mind Becky never left her. In her troubled mind the little girl who held her hand and told her things were all right was the same Becky she'd rocked to sleep as an infant.

Sal, of course, knew better.

Sal knew from the beginning that Beth wasn't his granddaughter, despite Nellie's protestations that she was.

Sal knew it was wrong to purchase Beth from Sanchez. Although Sanchez talked a good game about running an orphanage for children, Sal could see him for what he was.

A con man, through and through.

Sal was able to keep his guilt at bay by convincing himself that maybe the child was indeed an orphan. That Sanchez certainly was no advocate for her needs and certainly ran no orphanage.

But maybe, just maybe, if she really didn't have any parents, maybe he and Nellie could fill that role.

And certainly if she had parents, they'd have come running out of the house that day to prevent Sanchez' sale of the child to Sal and Nellie.

He also kept his feelings of guilt at bay by seeing the difference Beth had made in Nellie's life.

Beth made her smile for the first time in months.

Beth put the gleam back in Nellie's eyes.

Beth gave the old woman life once again.

Sal convinced himself that, regardless of the circumstances in which Beth came to live with them, it was better for all concerned.

Nellie became vibrant again. She was her old self once again.

The child was in good hands. Hands which would care for her and protect her. And keep her away from men like Sanchez.

And if Beth really did have living parents and a family back in Kansas... well, they should take solace in knowing that she was placed with a couple who'd do right by her.

After all, Sal had only Beth's word that her mother was decent and kind and cared for her.

For all Sal knew, the exact opposite might be true.

For all those reasons, Sal had felt little guilt and lost little sleep in knowing they'd purchased a human being and taken her away under nefarious means.

All that changed when Nellie died.

Sal no longer had to pretend he'd legally adopted the child.

And the guilt finally hit him hard, like a sledge hammer.

Then the depression. As though Nellie's death wasn't bad enough.

He'd kept it a secret from everyone else in the compound. Sure, Beth wasn't shy about telling the other children, and even some of the adults, that she wasn't really Sal's granddaughter. That her name wasn't really Becky. That she had her own family somewhere else.

Sal had countered her claims merely by denying them. He said she was merely a troubled child who'd suffered a lot of trauma in seeing her family murdered in front of her. That her claims were just the acts of a lonely child who was desperate for love and attention and sympathy.

Sal's brother Benny was one of the few adults in the compound who knew the truth.

For he'd known Becky.

And he knew that Beth wasn't her.

"What are you going to do with her?" he'd asked Sal several days after Nellie was laid to rest.

"I honestly don't know," Sal had replied. "I suppose I could take her back to Kansas City. To return her to the place where I got her. But the trip was so harsh. And I'm so old. I'm not sure I could make that journey again. And I'm still not sure the situation she's in now isn't better than the one she was in. I mean, the man she calls Sanchez... he was an evil one through and through. I could see it the moment I set eyes upon him. A big part of me thinks she's better off here than going back to that man, who might do God-knows-what to her."

It was, of course, rationalization in a classic form.

But it made it much easier to justify in his own mind why it would be easier and better for all concerned to just leave Beth where she was.

"Besides," Sal continued, "I'm not even sure I could find that place again if I did take her back. When we found it we were just wandering around in the dark looking for a horse to buy, not paying much attention to road signs or landmarks. I might take her back on a fool's journey, unable to reunite her.

"I think she's better off here. I can still raise her and provide for her, just as well as anyone back there could."

Benny, for his part, was a God fearing Christian man. He didn't like any of it, although he tried very hard to understand his brother's reasoning for buying the girl.

Sal looked to Benny for advice, and got an earful.

"You've got to take her aside and apologize to her. Explain to her that it was wrong to purchase her. That you know that now. That you were blinded by your desire to make Nellie happy.

"You've also got to explain to her that you're sorry. That you did a very bad thing, but that you cannot take her back. But that the least you can do is admit to one and all she's not your granddaughter. That her name really is Beth. And that she came to you under the worst of circumstances.

"Then you must tell her that even though you cannot take her back, that you'll raise her as your own. That she'll want for nothing. That in time her former family will become just a distant memory, and that she'll learn to accept and love her new family.

"She won't like it. And neither of us can blame her. But under the circumstances she'll have little choice but to accept it.

"This blackout has been hell on all of us, in different ways. We've got people living amongst us who have lost every relative they ever had.

"It may sound very harsh, but this child is better off than many. At least she'll grow up knowing her family was still alive when she last saw them. It'll give her hope that maybe when she's grown, the world will be a different place than it is today. Perhaps in her lifetime people will be able to get about easier. Perhaps in her lifetime she'll be able to go back and find her first family, if that's what she desires.

"Tell her that. It'll give her hope and help sustain her in the months and years ahead.

"And tell her in the meantime you'll protect and provide for her, just as though she really was Becky.

"Answer me this, Sal. Do you love this child?"

"Yes. Yes, I do. We started out on rocky footing. But she's grown on me. She's a special child in so many ways. And yes, I love her."

"Then go to her. Tell her you're sorry for the circumstances which brought you two together. Tell her you believed Sanchez. That you thought you were legally adopting her. Make her understand you had only her best interests in mind.

"Tell her that you love her and will raise her as your own daughter. That you'll provide for her and protect her. And that you'll never, ever let anyone take her away again."

## Chapter 55

Two down.

Dave didn't know how many more he'd have to kill before the vengeance he felt for Tony was satisfied. But he was up to the task.

The rain was letting up a bit now. It was as though the skies couldn't make up their minds whether they wanted to rain or not.

Or perhaps they were just trying to mess with Dave's mind.

He saw the rain as an ally. It made it far easier to move from one point to another without being seen. It would have been nice if it were more consistent. But hey, he shouldn't complain. It was what it was. When it rained heavily, he'd move around quicker. When it slowed, he'd slow as well. Either way he'd make darned sure he didn't do anything stupid which would get himself killed.

For that would doom Beth to a lifetime of servitude. And she deserved far better than that.

He made his way back to the burned house. His base of operations.

There were a couple of walls still partially standing. Across them half a sheet of sheetrock, its edges broken and jagged. But it provided a limited amount of relief from the rain while he pondered his next move.

Before he left his first two victims he thought to check them for radios. He wanted to be able to monitor the enemy's movements. And to know as soon as his presence was discovered.

Neither of the men had a radio.

Dave was pleased. That would make things much easier for him.

It meant he could move at will as long as he was quiet.

The enemy had very little discipline. They apparently thought they'd melt in the rain and were likely staying indoors. They were very unlikely to spot him from their windows as long as he stayed a respectable distance from the houses.

As long as he didn't encounter any additional checkpoints along the way… checkpoints which weren't there two nights before, he should be able to return to Dalton's headquarters without any trouble.

He went through his weapons bag and selected his weapons for the next round.

Two hand grenades. His crossbow, which was already serving him well. And which had no appreciable drop due to the rain. His AR-15 and handgun.

Of course, his knife was still strapped to his boot and would be for the remainder of his campaign.

The knife and crossbow would be his primary weapons if he encountered any more bad guys on his way to the headquarters house.

He needed to be as stealthy as possible for as long as possible.

Because as soon as the first shot was fired, everything would change.

He felt in his pocket for Tony's hand drawn map and it wasn't there.

He'd lost the damn thing. It had fallen out somewhere along the way.

It wasn't a major problem, though.

It was an easy route to remember.

However… if he lost it in enemy territory, and if Dalton's people found it, they'd know for sure how he got in and out the first time he was here.

And they'd likely set up men along the route to stop him from coming back the same way.

Perhaps even set booby traps for him.

"Damn it," he muttered under his breath.

He hated it when he did something stupid.

He used to tell his Marines, "Stupid isn't just embarrassing, it's deadly. Stupid gets you and your buddies killed."

He should have listened better to his own sermon.

He stuck to the center of the alley, the center of the streets, as he made his way by memory back to the headquarters building.

The rain hadn't let up. It was still coming down in buckets, still his friend and ally.

## Chapter 56

Just when Dave started thinking the odds were on his side, that this was easier than he thought it would be, an old nemesis returned.

The lightning.

He was within sight of the boarded up gas station now, perhaps eighty yards from it, when the sky lit up brilliantly for almost a full second.

His instincts took over and he was on the ground immediately, temporarily unable to see anything.

Night vision goggles work by amplifying light.

The flash from a lightning bolt as seen through such goggles can be blinding and almost painful.

As he waiting for his vision to return, he did two things: he ripped the goggles from his face, and he rolled toward a minivan he'd seen to his left just before the flash.

The first act was to prevent his being blinded again by the next flash.

The second was to get behind some kind of shelter. Any kind, to prevent him from being shot if he was spotted.

Anyone paying attention during the first flash would have seen him. They'd have noted his position, set up their shot, and easily picked him off on the next flash.

He turned the goggles off and would do without them for the time being.

The next flash came a full minute later, and he counted the interval between the lightning and the thunder which followed it.

Four seconds. The storm's center was still some distance away. That meant the rain would soon get heavier, the lightning flashes more severe, the cracks of thunder louder.

About seventy yards away, directly in front of the boarded up gas station, was an elevated Chevy

Silverado. It was a flat black in color, almost impossible to see on a dark night even with goggles, as it blended in well with the dark blue painted walls of the gas station.

But the second lightning strike lit it up like a Christmas tree.

Just as it had Dave.

And that was the thing. Dave once had a Silverado of the same year, and almost the same color. It wasn't jacked up, but other than that the silhouette was familiar to him.

He passed a lot closer to the station the first time he came through here. If the truck had been there then, it would have caught his eye.

Because he loved that old truck. He'd owned it for years and never had a lick of trouble with it. It was the most dependable truck he'd ever owned. He only got rid of it because he and Sarah had decided they didn't need three vehicles for a two-driver household. As the oldest vehicle they had, the truck was the logical sacrifice. Dave sold it on Craig's List and never saw it again. But damn, he sure missed it. More than most of the women he'd once dated, more than any other vehicle he'd ever traded or sold.

If it had been there two nights before he'd have noticed.

He didn't know where it came from. But somebody had rolled it to the station from somewhere. Probably the driveway of a nearby house.

Dave wasn't a rocket scientist. Never claimed to be one. But he knew a little bit about geometry.

He used to joke with Sarah that the high schools put way too much emphasis on math skills. It was his hardest subject and he'd struggled with math each and every day in school.

"I don't know why they torture the kids the way they do," he'd said when Lindsey brought home a C in math. "I've lived my whole life so far, and no one... I mean no one, has ever asked me to solve an algebraic equation or do a geometry problem."

"Oh, Dave," she'd patiently said as she rolled her eyes. "You use geometry all the time. You just don't know it."

"Oh yeah? Give me just one example. Just one."

"Every time you shoot pool, you use geometry. You line up your bank shot by trying to figure out the precise place to bounce your cue ball off the rail and then to knock your ball into the pocket. That, my friend, is geometry."

It gave him pause. But not for long.

"Okay. I'll admit you're right about geometry. But prove me wrong about algebra."

Sarah thought, then said, "I can't. No one has ever asked me to solve an algebraic equation either. You win."

"Ha! They should save that foolishness for college, and then only teach it to people who want to be doctors and scientists and stuff. Let kids be kids and have more fun in high school."

The truth was, Dave was just happy to win an argument with his wife. He very seldom did.

Why he thought about that particular conversation at that particular time, he had no idea.

Then he realized he was using geometry again, this time to estimate the rough angle from his position when the lightning lit him up in the street, as viewed from the windshield of the black Silverado.

Specifically, he was trying to determine whether the men sitting in the pickup could have seen him from their particular point of view.

And he determined they couldn't have seen him. Their vantage point was blocked by two other vehicles between their position and Dave's.

Good old geometry. It was all of a sudden Dave's best friend. He suddenly wished he'd taken more of it.

But not more algebra. Screw that.

From the angle he was at, though, they could just make out a shadowy figure on the ground next to the minivan. If they were paying closer attention than the fools at the Town Car were.

He crawled back a bit to lessen the size of his profile, and put the crossbow off to the side.

The AR-15 rifle had been slung over his shoulder. He took it off and aimed it in the general direction of the Silverado.

And he waited.

## Chapter 57

As Dave saw it, the men in the pickup had no radios. If working radios were available, they'd have given the first set to the clowns working the Town Car. They were at the entrance to the Dalton's Raiders' turf, and therefore presumably the first line of defense.

The fact they didn't have radios told Dave nobody else would either.

That only left two problems. They were sizeable, but not insurmountable.

The first was the shots.

Dave wouldn't be able to use the crossbow for this part of his operation.

While a crossbow bolt might go through a thin glass pane window at, say, a residential house, and remain true to its course, thick auto glass was a different story.

A sloped windshield would deflect the bolt. It might veer off without penetrating the glass at all. If it did break through, it certainly wouldn't follow its original path.

The side windows offered the same problem, but to a lesser degree.

The crossbow was out.

The bullet from a high powered rifle could conceivably be deflected as well. But it was far more likely to stay on course than the slower and longer bolt.

Luckily the Silverado's windshield was almost true vertical on that particular model. It wasn't as sloped as a lot of windshields. And that would help.

The other problem Dave faced was the noise from the shots themselves.

They wouldn't need radios. At the first sound of gunshots they'd scramble to find him and kill him. If they weren't already in war mode they soon would be.

Maybe.

Or maybe not.

The storm was a fast mover. It was almost directly overhead now. Dave could tell because the thunder was coming only a second or so after the lightning flashes now.

And it was louder. Much louder.

Dave had a plan. But to make it work he'd have to time everything perfectly.

And he'd have to be damn lucky.

The sky lit up again.

But it was a brief flash. Not enough to do him much good.

He'd need a much longer flash. A flash which extended for a second or more.

He lifted the cover to his rifle's scope and peered through it.

He couldn't see squat.

Then the sky lit up again, this time for a split second longer.

It gave him the opportunity to align his scope with the driver's side of the pickup, but wasn't long enough for him to make out whether there was anyone in it.

The third lightning bolt, twenty seconds later, gave him that opportunity.

A white male, in his twenties, was sitting in the driver's seat, smoking a cigarette and talking nonchalantly to a second man seated beside him.

Dave smiled.

He lined up his crosshairs on the man's heart. If the bullet deflected upward it would still hit him in the upper chest or throat. Both mortal wounds considering there were no trauma centers operating nearby. And they wouldn't waste valuable time and medicines on such a scumbag anyway.

To make his plan work he'd need to fire into the first man's chest, pivot quickly to his left, and fire a second round into the general area where he knew the second man to be.

And that was the problem. By the time he fired the second shot, the light would be gone. He'd have to get lucky. If he missed, the man would likely exit the vehicle and run.

Since he knew the area and Dave didn't, he'd likely get away to warn the others.

He said a quick prayer:

*Lord, I know you're all about not killing, and you try not to choose sides and all. But these men are vile and evil, and brutally murdered a good friend of mine. If you can see your way into helping me out just this once, I'd really appreciate it. Thank you, Lord. Amen.*

Then he went back to waiting.

It occurred to him he was getting pretty good at that.

The first lightning flash was too brief. The thunder that followed wasn't long enough.

The next was a bit longer. But not long enough.

So he waited. Thirty seconds. Then a minute. All the while the rain was beating down upon him.

He tried to focus on the fundamentals. Breath control. Trigger control. He rested the pad of his finger on the trigger, ready not to pull, but to squeeze.

The prone position was his best firing stance. It was from the prone position he'd earned the marksmanship ribbon in the Marines. Twice.

And this, despite the heavy rain, was a much closer shot.

In the Corps he'd fired the M-16, which was the military version of the weapon he held in his hands. They were almost identical, except for the full-auto feature the M-16 had. He wished he had the feature now. But then again, he'd seldom use full auto even if he did have it. It tended to expend a lot of ammo, and there would come a day when ammunition would be more valuable than gold or silver.

His thoughts were drifting. He refocused.

At last, the sky lit up in a brilliant flash of lightning that lasted more than a second. It struck something close by. The following thunder would be deafening. And that was perfect for his needs.

In the flash of light he zeroed in once again on his target: the heart of the man in the driver's seat.

By the time the thunder rumbled, he could no longer see his target.

But he knew where he was.

He squeezed off the first shot and then pivoted slightly to where he estimated the second man would be.

And he squeezed off two more quick shots.

He was almost too slow. The final shot came just as the thunder was ending.

But he was right. The roar of the thunder was deafening and covered the shots completely.

He held his breath and got ready to move.

If the second man got away he'd be off on a mad scramble to find him. To catch him before he could warn the others.

He'd have to leave his crossbow and rifle behind. For their battle wouldn't be with firearms. It would be hand-to-hand. Dave would have to get the upper hand, and then he'd shove his knife with all his strength through the man's sternum and through his heart.

He was ready to bolt.

But he didn't have to.

When the lightning flashed again it once again lit up the cab of the Silverado for a second or so.

That wasn't long in the grand scheme of things.

But it was long enough to reveal to Dave a truly macabre sight.

The man in the driver's seat was killed instantly. Dave's first shot was true and deadly.

He slumped to his right, his eyes and mouth wide open.

The man in the passenger seat lived a split second longer. That was apparent because he died with a look of pain on his face the first man didn't have.

He slumped to his left.

Both men's heads were touching, in what some might have interpreted as two lovers saying goodbye.

Dave didn't know whether they were lovers, friends, or whether they hated each other's guts.

It didn't matter to him at all.

They were dead.

And that was good enough for him.

## Chapter 58

Dave knew not to get cocky. He'd come against four men and killed them all. He was four and oh.

His confidence was building. But confidence was healthy. Cockiness could be deadly.

In Fallujah five years before, Dave and his men had a fierce firefight with a handful of insurgents. The bad guys were pinned behind the rubble of a stone and mud building, and had fought ferociously.

Finally, all fell silent behind the ruins, and a good friend and fellow lance corporal stood up to celebrate.

"Yeah!" he yelled. "Take that, you slimy bastards!"

He took a round to the face.

Dave had gone with the man on the medivac helicopter. He didn't return to the scene until hours later.

One of his men showed him what became of the shooter.

There wasn't much left of him, after he'd been riddled with a hundred bullets and a Marine in a Hummer rolled over his body several times.

An embedded photographer took a photo which showed up in a major weekly magazine a few weeks later. An investigation was started and went nowhere.

The United States Marine Corps has a very long and very proud history.

Part of that history is their belief that a fellow Marine is closer than a brother. Closer than a mother or a father.

He who is insane enough to accost a fellow Marine will pay a heavy price. If possible, the ultimate price.

The dead Iraqi was soon forgotten. The photographer who took the photo and sent it off to be published was transferred to another unit.

A non-combat unit.

He wasn't in danger, mind you.

He was just no longer welcome.

As for the man who drove back and forth over the dead man's body a dozen or so times, he was never identified.

For every man in the outfit happened to be somewhere else at the time, and every man in the outfit had at least three of his buddies to vouch for him.

The lieutenant colonel tasked with conducting the investigation had a heart to heart talk with the lieutenant in charge of the operation.

"How is it that none of your men saw what happened to that dead asshole, lieutenant?"

"They were doing what I ordered them to do, sir. They were to seek out more insurgents and watch each other's backs."

"I see. Well, it sounds like they did an especially good job of watching each other's backs."

"Yes sir. I suppose they did."

"Did your men learn anything from this endeavor, lieutenant?"

"I suspect so, but not as much as the insurgents."

"Meaning?"

"I suspect if there were any other insurgents watching, they learned not to mess with the United States Marine Corps."

"It looks like I'm finished here. Semper Fi, lieutenant."

"Semper Fi, sir."

Dave's friend, the one who was shot, survived. But he would be horribly disfigured for the rest of his life, as half his jaw was blown away.

Dave wouldn't see him again for several months, after his own return to the States.

The man was at Walter Reed Medical Center, recovering after his fifth reconstructive surgery.

"How you doin', Tom?"

"Oh, I'm okay, Dave. Not quite as handsome as I once was, but still better looking than you. Welcome home."

"Thanks. I wish I didn't have to see you again like this."

"Don't waste your pity on me, Dave. I'm one of the lucky ones. There are twelve men just on this ward who've lost one or more limbs. Seven more with spinal injuries. At least I've got all my parts left."

Dave was amazed at his spirit. And he repeated the lieutenant colonel's now-famous question.

"Did you learn anything, Tom?"

"Yes. I learned not to stand up until we're damn sure the battle's over. It was a stupid move."

Dave couldn't argue.

"Yes it was, my friend. Yes it was."

"Dave, do you think that someday they'll quit sending us over there to fight senseless wars, just because people can't learn to get along?"

Dave pondered the question before answering.

"I'd like to say yes, Tom. But you and I know better. As long as congressmen don't have to send their own sons to die, and as long as the powerful men who own those congressmen make billions of dollars on the war machine, they'll keep sending us over there to fight and die. It's been that way for a long time, and I expect it'll stay that way."

"Semper Fi, my friend."

"Semper Fi."

Yes, cockiness could be deadly.

And Dave would learn from his friend's mistake.

He would proceed with caution and would assume two things:

That there would be others watching out for him. Others that might not be so easy to spot.

And that his third shot, coming at the end of the thunderclap, was identifiable as a gunshot.

He had to assume that all over Crazy Town people were saying to one another, "Did you hear that? It sounded like a gunshot," and were acting accordingly.

From here on out, he couldn't count on being so lucky.

So he had to make his own luck.

## Chapter 59

The storm front was directly above him now, the prudent thing waiting for it to pass. As long as lightning lit the sky several times a minute, the goggles were useless.

It was one of two advantages he'd had coming in, the other being the rain to hide his movements and provide him the advantage of surprise.

Now the rain was just becoming a pain in the ass.

He was starting to shiver, his clothes were drenched, and he still had a long way to go.

He crawled into the back of a UPS truck and sprawled across several boxes, then closed his eyes.

Not because he was sleepy, but because there was really nothing to look at while he waited out the storm.

At least the rain wasn't beating directly upon his head.

The minutes ticked by slowly, seeming like hours.

He tried to kill time by going over in his mind what his next move might be.

The truth was, he had no plan.

A plan would have required information he just flat didn't have. Like how many more sentries were out there. And how well fortified the headquarters was. And how much firepower they had.

"Playing it by ear" was fine for musicians. But it really sucked as a battle plan.

He checked his watch. It was almost two hundred hours. Two a.m. He was glad the watch was waterproof, but wished it was a bit earlier. He'd hoped to be at the headquarters raging a bloody battle by now, so he could get the hell out of Dodge before the sun came up.

By two thirty he decided it was time to go. It was still raining, but the lightning storm had passed him by. The only thunder he heard was far in the distance, and the occasional lightning flash was dim and weak. Not bright enough to blind him, even if he looked directly at it through the goggles.

He put them back onto his head and scanned the area first, before stepping back into the muck.

Nothing. He had his advantage back. He could see in the dark, and his opponents couldn't.

His confidence began to return.

He made his way carefully, from one abandoned car to the next, until he was within a hundred yards or so of the headquarters house.

There, in one of the front yards on the side of the street thirty yards ahead of him, was what appeared to be a statue.

Only it wasn't a statue.

It was a man, in military woodland camouflage, standing at parade rest.

Not moving a muscle.

Just standing there.

He had to be prior military. Otherwise he wouldn't have had the presence of mind and self-discipline to stand there in the heavy rain.

Dave hated to shoot a fellow military man. But this man stood in the way of his objective. And he was on the wrong side.

He charged his cross bow and prepared to take aim.

But something was wrong.

He couldn't put a finger on it.

The man was just… too still.

Even a man at parade rest twitched now and then. Adjusted his stance so his legs didn't fall asleep and his knees didn't lock. After watching the man for a full five minutes Dave hadn't gotten an indication of movement. Not at all.

Then the wind changed direction and Dave caught just a whiff of a now familiar smell.

It was the smell of burned flesh, tempered by the rain but still quite pungent.

And he realized what was wrong.

The figure before him wasn't a former soldier.

It was a former friend.

He checked his surroundings again before moving forward.

"Oh, Tony... what in the hell did they do to you?"

The men were mad. They had to be. They'd taken the body of his friend and dressed him in BDUs, a battle dress uniform, then impaled him on an eight foot long stake, driven into the ground.

As a final insult he was posed, his body contorted into a position of parade rest so precise it would have made any soldier proud.

He wondered what kind of insanity would make men do such a thing to a once living, once breathing human being.

A man who never did a damn thing to them.

They'd obviously noticed that Dave had moved Tony from the street and deposited him beneath the tree. It wasn't much of a gesture, really, but in Dave's mind it was a more dignified place for Tony to rest.

They'd also obviously figured out that only a friend of Tony's would make such a gesture.

So although they'd never met Dave, and couldn't have picked him out of a lineup, they were on to him. They knew that the man who'd moved Tony from the street would be back for revenge.

Whether they hung Tony's body like a macabre scarecrow to inflame him, to goad him into being outraged and getting sloppy, was one possibility.

Another was that they were simply insane, as Tony had contended, and gave no thought to the matter.

Maybe they just liked to put their victims on display, in the same manner some of the other factions posted the heads of their enemies on sticks for all the world to see.

Maybe in CrazyTown they just went one step further.

Whatever the reason, Dave was incensed.

But if they were counting on that to make him careless or make him rush headlong into something he shouldn't he'd disappoint them.

He'd keep his cool head.

He thought about taking the body down under the cover of rain and darkness, but decided against it.

Tony was in a better place now, free of pain. He was sure of that.

His body was nothing but an empty vessel now. Whether it was upright on a stick, skewered like a shish-kabob or lying on the muddy ground no longer mattered. Tony's spirit, Dave was certain, wouldn't have cared either way.

He passed his friend by and continued to make his way to the Daltons' HQ.

## Chapter 60

He finally reached his objective a bit after four a.m., as the rain was starting to let up a bit.

He hoped it didn't stop completely. If it did, the cloud cover might blow over, following the storm to the east.

And if that happened, if the stars and moon became visible once again, he'd lose much of his cover.

From some heavy bushes, across the street and two houses down, Dave watched the Dalton house for any sign of movement.

As was the case two nights before, the lights were on inside the house.

Only this time, the heavy drapes were open in the big picture window on the front porch.

That was odd. Very odd.

Even as crazy as the bunch was, they had to know that the open drapes lit them up like fish in a barrel for anyone outside with a rifle.

And indeed, Dave was incredulous to see people walking around, laughing, and having what appeared to be a good time.

He wondered whether they were still using Tony's stash of drugs. Whether they'd been on the same bender since the last time he'd seen them.

Dave didn't know a lot about illicit drugs. He learned a little bit in the Marine Corps, so he could tell whether any of his men started using. He learned more from Tony, who'd described the various drugs he peddled and how they affected people.

Tony had told him most of his customers in Crazy Town were meth junkies. Speed. And that the meth they smoked or injected into their veins made them stay awake for days at a time. They lost their appetite and their sense of thirst, and simply had no desire to rest or sleep. Their bodies began to twitch almost uncontrollably and they began to hallucinate. They became very paranoid and irrational. And sometimes they felt invincible.

Maybe invincible enough to think the incompetent sentries they put out were enough to take care of their Dave problem.

Maybe invincible enough not to care whether the blinds were open or closed.

Maybe invincible enough not to notice, or not to care, that they were all like the targets at a carnival midway game, just waiting for Dave to pick them off one at a time.

He watched the house for maybe half an hour before deciding it was safe to go further.

Then it took him a full five minutes to work his way to the front of the house, where he hid in the bushes just outside the picture window.

The same idiots who were part of the party two nights before were at it again. Only this time they looked more zoned out than before.

Dave wondered if the party had gone non-stop for two days.

"Damn, Tony," he muttered under his breath. "How much dope were you carrying in that satchel of yours, anyway?"

At one point, Dave thought he was busted when two of the men approached the window and stared intently through it.

They looked as though they were on their own planet, and they peered directly at Dave.

He thought his goose was cooked.

But it turned out the tweakers couldn't see anything except their reflections in the glass of the lighted room. They were debating about whether their faces were melting.

Dave worked his way around to the back of the house and peered over a privacy fence.

He was overjoyed to see that the back door, and all the windows on the rear of the house, had been boarded over with plywood.

He wondered why.

Perhaps to save themselves the trouble of guarding the rear of the house, maybe?

In any event, the only point of escape was through the front door.

This was too good to be true. He must be dreaming.

But he wasn't.

Dalton's Raiders might have been mean beyond compare and absolutely ruthless when it came to dealing with their enemies.

But they knew nothing about the art of war. They were the lousiest tacticians Dave had ever encountered.

And he'd make sure they paid for it dearly.

## Chapter 61

The rain had slowed to a drizzle. That was the only thing working to Dave's disadvantage. He wanted the additional cover the rain would provide, especially as he made his egress from the Dalton's compound.

And time began to become critical. He checked his watch again. It was almost oh four thirty.

Ordinarily he could count on the sun rising around five thirty or so. And that would still happen regardless of the rain. But the additional darkness the heavy rain clouds would provide would make it much easier to get out of there unmolested.

But that wasn't a problem. He'd be wrapped up in an hour and on his way back to the freeway.

By noon he'd be bunked out in a sleeper cab, catching up on his sleep.

And by midnight he'd be on his way west from Albuquerque, resuming his desperate search for little Beth.

Of course, none of that was going to happen. Not the way he expected it to, anyway.

For things had gone way too smoothly to this point. It was time for something to go wrong.

Dave looked around along the side of the house for something heavy. A big rock. A brick. A crescent wrench. Hell, he didn't care what it was. As long as it was heavy enough to break glass.

And there it was, on the ground not far from his feet. A broken red brick, twice the size of his fist.

"Hot damn!"

He couldn't believe his good fortune.

He took the brick back to the front of the house and returned to his previous hiding place, directly in front of the expansive picture window.

And there he waited for the rain to start again.

He figured he'd wait until oh five hundred. If the rain didn't come back by then he'd have to go without it. But he'd still have at least half an hour to clear the territory before the sky began to lighten.

Dave felt confident.

No, he was starting to feel a little bit cocky.

And he should have known better.

For he wasn't aware that four men were bearing down on his location, two blocks away and moving stealthily toward him. These men weren't like any he'd encountered in the compound thus far. They were well trained and disciplined. They had the know how and experience to match Dave's own.

They were, by anybody's estimation, formidable opponents.

He'd also underestimated the quality of his watch. He'd noticed it was still ticking even after he spent hours in a drenching rain.

But it was ticking at a far slower rate than it should have been, losing almost twenty minutes per hour.

Dave's good luck was starting to turn. And he hadn't a clue.

He sat in the bushes in front of the house, glancing upward at the sky every few minutes.

He'd erred in keeping the goggles in place too long, and assumed the bright light he saw to be the goggles doing their job.

It wasn't until he finally took off the goggles that he noticed the sun was already rising. The sky was becoming lighter, and his cover of darkness was pretty much gone.

"Shit."

It wasn't a word he used often, but under the circumstances no other word would do.

He looked around and saw no movement, nothing amiss.

He'd blown it. Big time. He didn't know what happened. His watch said five after five.

But it was what it was. He couldn't go back, and he couldn't change anything.

His only option was to press ahead and hope for the best.

He'd never thrown a grenade through a glass window before. He assumed that at close distance, thrown hard enough, it would shatter the glass and fall into the room full of miscreants.

But if the glass was heavier than it appeared, or if the window was double paned, or if his throw wasn't strong enough, it might bounce right off the window and back into the bushes with him.

He couldn't take that chance.

Hence, the much heavier brick.

He held the grenade in his left hand, took a deep breath, and heaved the brick with his right.

The plate glass shattered, spraying glass everywhere, and causing heads to turn all over the house.

Their heads turned, but they were too stoned or too stupid to respond in any other way. Most of them were carrying side arms, but nobody drew them.

Most of them didn't even dive for cover when the grenade came rolling into the room a couple of seconds later. They were either too high to see it or confused as to what to do.

The blast took out several of them outright.

Several more would die within hours, for there were simply no trauma facilities in the area equipped to handle blast injuries and shrapnel wounds.

Dave's second grenade went a little farther into the room and took out a couple more.

The second blast got a better response from the survivors, who kept their heads down and searched for cover.

And that gave Dave time to pull back and take a position behind a heavy oak tree in the neighbor's yard.

The tree was forked at shoulder height and gave Dave an excellent place to rest the barrel of his rifle as he took aim at the front door.

As he'd expected, the drug-addled survivors couldn't wait to leave the house that seemed to be blowing up around them. Even if it meant evacuating in the very direction the grenades had come from.

Tweakers high as a kite on crystal meth, who'd been up for several days, weren't the most logical thinkers around.

The first two came running out the door, bloody and confused.

Dave sent them both to hell with two shots each to their respective torsos.

Dave didn't see that behind him, behind the cover of a solid steel and very heavy 1963 Chevy Impala, four men also raised their weapons in Dave's direction.

The next one out the door was Dalton himself.

He wasn't wounded, and had come stumbling down the stairs following the second blast.

Of course, Dave had never laid eyes on the man who'd ordered Tony's murder. He didn't have a clue who he was.

But he pulled the trigger anyway.

And the funniest thing happened.

Dalton wasn't just hit once, by Dave's bullet.

Dalton was torn apart by automatic weapons fire.

And not just by one automatic weapon.

He was cut down by several. It was the first time Dave had heard several weapons firing on full auto since he left Fallujah.

The fire came from behind him, between him and the tree he was using as cover.

He immediately went to the dirt. It was really the only option he had.

Dave wouldn't even realize until later he'd peed his pants as he quickly low-crawled to the only shelter he had available to him: a low brick wall twenty yards away.

He covered the distance in record time, although from his point of view it seemed much farther than it really was. From his point of view it seemed like miles.

## Chapter 62

Dave was in a tight spot and knew it.

He had no time to regroup. Combat didn't allow one the pleasure of relaxing and thinking things through.

Luckily the United States Marine Corps was well aware of that fact, and trained their Marines constantly.

So they reacted to a situation without thinking much about it.

Dave had no idea what had just happened. Or, more to the point, what was still happening. For the automatic weapons fire continued in short bursts.

Not directed in Dave's direction, something he was extremely grateful for.

But rather toward the Dalton house.

There were more hand grenades too. Whoever was in the process of assaulting the Dalton's headquarters was extremely well armed.

He didn't want to, and he knew full well he was risking getting his head blown off.

But he had to peek over the wall. He couldn't afford to let himself get pinned down behind the wall against such firepower. He had to see where the shooters were so he could quickly egress without running headfirst into their midst.

What he saw were four men dressed in Army-issue desert cammies. They were now in the front yard of the Dalton house, spraying every part of it with short bursts of gunfire. Expending vast amounts of ammunition.

Whoever this bunch was, they apparently didn't like the Daltons much.

But more importantly to Dave, they were temporarily distracted and had their backs to him.

Dave took the opportunity to skirt the wall and get the hell out of Dodge. He kept his head low and zig-zagged from one abandoned car to another until he was a full block away

As he got farther away he heard the unmistakable pop of an incendiary grenade. He imagined the house would be fully engulfed in flames in a matter of minutes, and much as he'd love to go back and roast marshmallows while the rest of the Daltons were incinerated, he needed very much to be somewhere else.

And he got there as quickly as possible.

The streets were eerily quiet, even though it was fully light now. He'd expected to see reinforcements running toward the sound of the gunfire.

He was expecting to come under fire himself, as he expected to be immediately identifiable as an outsider.

But he saw not a soul on his way out of the compound.

Well, no live souls, anyway. He did pass by the two men in the Silverado pickup he'd shot, and the two at the Town Car.

And as a bonus, he saw the body of a man lying in the road with his throat cut. The body was so fresh it still had bright red blood oozing from the wound.

Dave suspected he was killed by the same band of men who were still shooting up the Dalton house.

He'd never know where the strange men had come from or why they were there.

He didn't know that word quickly got around to the other factions that the Daltons had murdered their neutral drug dealer.

And that the other factions were incensed about it.

Most of them grumbled and cursed about it, but didn't plan any type of revenge. They were reluctant to go to war with the inhabitants of Crazy Town.

But there was one faction, the Aryan Brotherhood, who just could not accept such a personal affront.

Their military wing, made up of Army and Marine combat veterans, was asked to do something to send a strong message to the Daltons.

They'd actually gone in as emissaries. They were to stop at the gate to the compound and demand to see Dalton himself. And they were to demand reparations of Dalton, in the form of territory.

The Brotherhood bordered Crazy Town on the north side. They were to demand most of Dalton's territory, in exchange for letting the Daltons continue to live.

Their thinking was that by reducing the Daltons' territory to just a couple of square miles, the rogue group would be weakened and it would be easier to wipe them out when the time came.

The Brotherhood had made a brilliant strategic move in the early days of the blackout when they raided the National Guard Armory. They had many things the other factions thirsted for but would never get. Things like automatic weapons, grenades, smoke and incendiary bombs and even land mines.

And about half a ton, by weight, of ammunition.

And as great as that was, perhaps one of the more useful things they obtained from the armory was a brand new set of radios, protected from electromagnetic pulse damage, complete with spare batteries, chargers and a base station.

The Brotherhood didn't realize how valuable the radios were until the four emissaries happened upon the Town Car and the two dead sentries.

They didn't know who'd assaulted the compound ahead of them or why. But the bodies were fresh and there was a good chance the incursion was still in progress.

They'd called in for guidance.

The Aryan Council conferred for only a couple of minutes before responding:

"We're going to get blamed for it anyway. Go in. Do them as much damage as you possibly can."

At the Dalton house, the four spotted Dave long before he saw them. They could have taken him out in a flash, but were intrigued by him. He was assaulting the house ahead of them.

They didn't know who he was or what faction he belonged to. But they viewed him as an ally.

And that saved Dave's life. That was why they passed him by and let him live to fight another day.

Dave made it back to the Polaris and high-tailed it away from the highway and to the safety of open ground.

He was immensely confused as to what transpired.

But he'd escaped with his ass intact when he should have been dead.

In the grand scheme of things, the cross bow he left behind seemed like a very small sacrifice to make.

**************************

**Thank you for reading**
## ALONE, Part 6: On Desert Sands

**Please enjoy this preview of**
## ALONE, Part 7: Payback

**************************

Dave almost never lost control. But on those rare occasions he did, it all went out the window: his sense of fairness, his sense of right or wrong.

And mostly, unfortunately, his empathy for another human being.

Sal managed to break free from Dave's grasp, but didn't get far. Dave threw a wild right hook that knocked the old man into the grass.

If Sal had been smarter he'd have stayed there.

Instead he tried to crawl away, and Dave was back on him in a flash.

Pummeling him, one blow after another.

Dave was in a blind rage. He had little control over his own body. And even less control over his mind.

He was not the kind of man who'd beat another when the other was down.

Nor the kind of man who'd beat senseless a man twice his age.

But he wasn't himself. The rage had turned him into a monster.

He saw only one thing. Knew only one truth:

This… this was the sadistic animal who took his little girl. This was the beast who turned her into a slave.

This was the bastard who may well have raped his child, or allowed others to do so.

This man must pay, and pay dearly, for what he did.

The man beneath him finally went limp. He was mercifully unconscious.

Dave didn't care. He wrapped both hands around Sal's throat and started to squeeze.

Sal's face turned blue. His eyelids were open, the eyeballs rolled back into their sockets.

Dave still didn't care.

He'd have kept squeezing. Kept it up until he could no longer feel the man's pulse. Kept it up until he finally felt satisfied that justice was done. That the man was duly punished.

That the man was on a fast train headed straight for the pits of hell.

Except…

Except for the plaintive cries of a little girl.

A little girl called Beth by most, Becky by others.

A little girl Dave hadn't seen in well over a year, yelling, "Daddy! Daddy! Stop it! You're killing him!"

It was only then that the glassiness left Dave's eyes. That he returned to the world of the living. That he became human again.

"Beth?"

He turned to look at his young daughter, now running at breakneck speed toward him.

He dropped Sal's head into the sand and stood up, then ran across the yard to meet her.

Old Sal, back from the brink where he'd been mere seconds from death, began to cough and to wheeze. Then he rolled to his right side and began to puke.

He was beaten bloody. But he'd survive.

Dave picked up the child and held her tight while blubbering like a baby.

He couldn't say a single word, but Beth filled the silence.

"You have it all wrong, Daddy. He wasn't mean to me. He took me, but it wasn't his fault. Sanchez told him I had no mommy or daddy. They thought they were adopting me.

"They were good to me, Daddy. They fed me and protected me and never made me do anything I didn't want to do.

"He's a good man, Daddy. He's grumpy sometimes, and I didn't used to like him much. But now he's my friend. Please don't hurt him anymore."

Now she was in tears too.

Dave was at a loss. For one of the few times in his life, he honestly didn't know what to do. He turned to look toward Sal, afraid it was too late. That he might already be dead.

He was relieved to see the old man sitting up.

He looked back to his daughter and asked, "Are you sure, honey?"

He hadn't felt the warmth of his daughter's embrace in a very long time. The last thing he wanted to do was to put her down.

But he was back. He was no longer just a lonely nobody wandering the highways of Southern California looking for his baby.

He, by God in heaven, was a father again.

And he needed to act like it.

He placed her gently back onto her feet and turned back toward Sal.

Sal saw him coming and wanted to run.

But he was too badly bruised. He was just barely conscious and feeling ready to pass out at any moment.

He did the only thing he was physically capable of doing.

He used his arms to cover his face and head and begged, "Please... please, don't hit me any more."

Dave went to one knee beside the old man and tenderly placed a hand upon his shoulder.

"I am so sorry, sir. Please forgive me for what I've done to you."

\*\*\*\*\*\*\*\*\*\*\*\*\*\*\*\*\*\*\*\*\*\*\*\*\*

# ALONE, Part 7:
# Payback

**will be available worldwide on Amazon.com and at Barnes and Noble Booksellers in April, 2017**

\*\*\*\*\*\*\*\*\*\*\*\*\*\*\*\*\*\*\*\*\*\*\*\*\*

\*\*\*\*\*\*\*\*\*\*\*\*\*\*\*\*\*\*\*\*\*\*\*\*

**Please enjoy this preview of
Darrell Maloney's new series**

# The Yellowstone Event, Book 1:
# FIRE IN THE SKY

**The Yellowstone Event series will premier
in January, 2017.**

\*\*\*\*\*\*\*\*\*\*\*\*\*\*\*\*\*\*\*\*\*\*\*\*

"Come on! What do you have to lose?" she cried gleefully as she dragged Tony by his arm through the midway.

"Um… how about ten bucks?"

"I'll give you a kiss."

"I'd rather keep the ten bucks."

"Excuse me, mister?"

He stopped and held her, then laughed.

"I'll tell you what. You give me just one good reason why I should throw away good money on a fortune teller. If you can give me just one good reason, I'll give in to your silly demands. But it'll still cost you a kiss."

"And what if I don't have a good reason? What if I'm just a silly girl who wants to find out once and for all whether you've been telling me the truth about marrying me someday?"

"Oh, so that's what this is all about. You're gonna make me pay ten of my hard-earned dollars just to hear some old gypsy fortune teller say what I've been telling you all along? That hurts. It really does."

"What hurts?"

"It hurts that you don't trust me. That you'd believe some crazy old fortune teller but you won't believe me."

"The fortune teller has nothing to gain by lying to me."

"And I do?"

"I don't know. Maybe."

"Maybe? Just what the heck does that mean, *maybe*?"

"It just means that you've been trying very hard to get to third base with me lately. And you wouldn't be the first guy who promised marriage to get the honeymoon first. That's all."

Tony smiled.

"Third base? Heck, baby. I don't want third base. I want a home run."

The smile left her face, replaced by something akin to a little girl's pout.

"You're not helping your case any."

He brushed the long brown hair from her face and kissed her on the tip of the nose. Then square on the lips.

"What if she's a fraud? Most of them are, you know. They just say whatever pops into their minds. They can no more tell the future than you or I can."

"I'll be able to tell if she's a fraud. If she is, I'll let you off the hook. But if she's genuine, I'll know that too."

"Oh, so now you're an expert on gypsy frauds?"

Her smile returned and she coyly replied, "Maybe."

"Oh, geez," he said as he stomped toward the purple tent. "The things I do to make you happy…"

"I know, honey. That's why I love you so very much."

She wasn't quite what he expected, when she sat them at the table. For one thing, she looked… normal. She wasn't the hideous witch he'd expected to find. She didn't have hair growing from weird warts on her nose and huge silver hoop earrings. There weren't bats flying around her head and the smell of cheap incense permeating everything in the tent.

She looked as normal as Tony and Hannah.

That sealed it in Tony's mind. That proved she was a fraud. She didn't even know enough to dress the part of a cartoonish gypsy. She didn't even put out that much effort. How much effort would she put into reading Hannah's emotions and verifying that yes, this guy sitting next to her was truly her one and only?

Now Tony could tell his own future. In about five minutes or so Hannah was going to go storming out of the tent and straight to the car. She'd insist that he take her home immediately. And once there she'd let herself out, slam the car door, and stomp her way up the steps to her house.

He'd be left in the car, his head still spinning, with absolutely no chance of getting lucky on this particular night.

"Good evening, Hannah. Good evening, Anthony. I've been wondering when you two were coming to call."

Hannah didn't catch it. She was too mesmerized by the woman's eyes. They were pools of blackness, devoid of emotion.

But Tony caught it. He'd always been good at that. At noticing subtle things others missed.

"How... how did you know our names?"

It was more of a demand than a question.

"Oh, I know more about you than that, young man. Stella knows everything about you. Your past, your present, your future. I know what's in your heart and what evil lurks hidden in your soul. I know the good in you. The bad. The secrets you keep. Now then, young man, the only question is, which things should I tell to Hannah and which ones do I keep to myself?"

His head told him she was bluffing, that she knew nothing about him. That maybe someone who knew them saw them coming and tipped her off to their names. Or that there was some other reasonable explanation.

His heart, it wasn't so sure.

"Relax, Anthony. You need not worry, for I know what's in your heart. This girl loves you. She wants to know if you love her as well. She wants to know if you'll marry her someday. It is a reasonable request. And I will share with her your true intentions."

Hannah's jaw dropped. Literally.

"But how…"

The gypsy placed a finger to her lips. Now was not the time for Hannah to speak. For she was about to receive the answer she'd been looking for.

Tony was on the hot seat. He overlooked the fact she'd called him Anthony. Nobody, but nobody, called him Anthony. He hated the name. He thought it made him sound like an accountant, slaving away in a cubicle with his calculator and his Buddy Holley glasses.

Forget all that. How in heck did she know why they went in there?

Tony looked at Hannah. Hannah looked back at him. Both of them suspected the other of sneaking in to talk to the woman beforehand.

And each of them could tell by the surprise on the other's face that they hadn't.

The gypsy turned her attention to Hannah.

"You are a beautiful girl, Hannah. You are desired by many boys. During your life you will be desired by many men. But at this place, at this time, your heart and your soul belong to only one man.

"You're here to find out if he feels the same way. You want to know if he will select you to be his bride. You want to know if he will father your children.

"The answer is yes. Yes to both questions. He will ask you to marry him, and he will be a good father to your children. He will be faithful and devoted to you. He will never stray.

"But…"

They had been gazing in each other's eyes. Hannah smiled as soon as she heard the gypsy's words. As hokey and improbable as it was, she had the confirmation she'd been looking for.

The "but..." stopped them short.

They immediately turned their attention back to the woman as she continued.

"But first, you must survive the great calamity. It will not be easy. You will be at great risk. Your loved ones and all of your friends will be in danger. Many of them will not make it.

"To earn your life together, to earn your children, you must survive the great calamity. You must help others to survive as well. Only then, as you walk away from the greatest death and destruction this country has ever seen, will you finally deserve the chance to become one."

Hannah could find no words.

Tony's head was swimming, trying to make sense of it all. But his tongue was still working.

"Great calamity? What great calamity? What in hell are you talking about?"

Hannah put her hand on his arm to calm him. She saw no reason for him to get ugly. No reason to curse at the woman.

But Tony wasn't angry.

Tony was confused.

"Beneath the great park they call Yellowstone lies death and destruction. It is well hidden and mostly unknown. But it is there. And you... both of you, will have the unique opportunity to save the lives of many.

"But... you must not marry until after the calamity is done. To do so will cause you distractions. You will be with child. You will lose your path, and your role in what fate hath wrought."

Hannah stammered, "What? What hath fate wrought?"

"The destruction of the United States of America."

Now Tony was starting to get angry.

"What in the hell are you talking about, you crazy old woman? What are you saying?"

The woman took the attack in stride, as though she fully expected it. She continued to meet his gaze and merely smiled at him.

Hannah took control, as she frequently did when Tony lost his cool.

"I think we'd better go," she said as she stood and pushed her chair back. Her hand was still on Tony's arm, and she fairly pulled him out of his own seat.

She turned back to the gypsy and said, "Thank you, ma'am."

The woman merely nodded, and continued to smile.

Hannah rushed Tony, who was now speechless, out of the tent and back onto the carnival midway.

They were fifty feet away when Hannah noticed the ten dollar bill still clutched in Tony's hand.

"Wait. We forgot to pay her."

"Screw her."

But Hannah was nothing if not honest. Bad karma came to those who took advantage of others.

She dragged him back to the tent and swept aside the flap.

The old gypsy was nowhere to be found.

## The Yellowstone Event, Book 1: FIRE IN THE SKY

**will be available on Amazon.com and at Barnes and Noble Booksellers in January, 2017.**

Made in the USA
Middletown, DE
19 May 2017